"I'm having a party tonight. Will you come?"

"I can't tonight. Also I should tell you I'm going steady with a boy from my school who is on this boat. We're a senior art and fashion class from Cleveland, and—"

Vic stands there staring at me.

"Why are we starting something that can't possibly go anywhere?"

Vic murmurs, "Trisha, it's because we're crazy— but a nice crazy!"

Caprice Romances from Tempo Books

DANCE WITH A STRANGER by *Elizabeth Van Steenwyk*
BEFORE LOVE by *Gloria D. Miklowitz*
SUNRISE by *G. C. Wisler*
THREE'S A CROWD by *Nola Carlson*
SOMEONE FOR SARA by *Judith Enderle*
S.W.A.K. SEALED WITH A KISS by *Judith Enderle*
CARRIE LOVES SUPERMAN by *Gloria D. Miklowitz*
PROGRAMMED FOR LOVE by *Judith Enderle*
A NEW LOVE FOR LISA by *Harriette S. Abels*
WISH FOR TOMORROW by *Pam Ketter*
THE BOY NEXT DOOR by *Wendy Storm*
A HAT FULL OF LOVE by *Barbara Steiner*
TWO LOVES FOR TINA by *Maurine Miller*
LOVE IN FOCUS by *Margaret Meacham*
DO YOU REALLY LOVE ME? by *Jeanne R. Lenz*
A BICYCLE BUILT FOR TWO by *Susan Shaw*
A NEW FACE IN THE MIRROR by *Nola Carlson*
TOO YOUNG TO KNOW by *Margaret M. Scariano*
SURFER GIRL by *Francess Lin Lantz*
LOVE BYTE by *Helane Zeiger*
WHEN WISHES COME TRUE by *Judith Enderle*
HEARTBREAKER by *Terry Hunter*
LOVE NOTES by *Leah Dionne*
NEVER SAY NEVER by *Ann Boyle*
THE HIDDEN HEART by *Barbara Ball*
TOMMY LOVES TINA by *Janet Quin-Harkin*
HEARTWAVES by *Deborah Kent*
STARDUST SUMMER by *Pam Ketter*
LAST KISS IN APRIL by *N. R. Selden*
SING A SONG OF LOVE by *Judith Enderle*

A CAPRICE ROMANCE

Last Kiss in April

N.R. Selden

TEMPO BOOKS, NEW YORK

LAST KISS IN APRIL

A Tempo Book / published by arrangement with
the author

PRINTING HISTORY
Tempo Original / April 1984

ISBN: 0-441-47119-6

"Caprice" and the stylized Caprice logo are trademarks
belonging to The Berkley Publishing Group.

Tempo Books are published by The Berkley Publishing Group,
200 Madison Avenue, New York, New York 10016.
Tempo Books are registered in the United States Patent Office.
PRINTED IN THE UNITED STATES OF AMERICA

Last Kiss in April

I'M CLINGING TO the rail of a ferryboat plowing toward the Statue of Liberty. The Statue of Liberty is actually a beige chocolate bar. I look around for Matt. Where is he? Beside me stands a strange boy who resembles Charlie Chaplin—sad eyes, black mustache, oversize shoes, funny black hat. Like a roller coaster the ferryboat climbs up the face of a huge wave. The boy pulls off his mustache. He's not handsome but his mouth is beautiful and his eyes are fascinating. We're sliding down the wave so fast I'm terrified. The Charlie Chaplin boy reaches out to break off a piece of the Statue of Liberty's torch. Where's Matt?

My alarm clock crashes the dream. I slap the blankets over my head. In the warm dark, I grab at the drifting pieces of leftover fantasy, but they dissolve like cubes of sugar in hot water.

Come on, Trisha, peel your face off the pillow! That may be Cleveland, Ohio outside your window now, but the Big Apple is waiting for you to take your first bite. Bus leaves in fifty minutes. We're heading for Manhattan this morning. Seniors from Ms. Garfield's art and fashion classes. My first time in New York—it's thrilling and silly and scary, going to a place you've only seen in magazines and movies, knowing it's the art and fashion center of the country. It seems like a place where anything could happen.

Would Matt be jealous if he knew this was the third time I dreamed about the Charlie Chaplin boy?

Trisha, you'll be late! Say goodbye to your blankets! Move it, girl!

I like to think about Matt. He has wonderfully shiny black hair and long, romantic eyelashes and a swimmer's body that excites me when I see him diving and racing for our school team, his arms and chest breaking from the water in the butterfly stroke. He's also a very talented artist and designer.

I wonder if he's awake, lying in bed like me, tasting the last traces of a dream. Or maybe he's in front of a mirror scraping a razor along the curve of his jaw.

I yawn. Paul Newman climbs up on my bed, rubbing his whiskers against my chin. He's hungry, I can tell, as I whisper like a parent to a child, "You'll have to wait."

He digs his claws affectionately into my arm. He's got a new red scratch on his neck from a fight with the orange cat next door.

"I wish I could take you with me to New York."

Paul Newman is getting old and it makes me sad.

"Trisha, you awake?" My mother's voice from downstairs.

"Yes, I am!"

"I'll be right up."

It bothers me, dreaming about the Charlie Chaplin boy. It's sort of disloyal to Matt.

Two bulging green suitcases stand at attention near my closet, stuffed with every item I need to dazzle Manhattan with my stylishness.

I laugh at myself taking this trip so seriously. New York, big deal! Who wants to breathe 95 percent factory smoke, get guns stuck in your ribs every other night, see nine million people stepping on each other! So what if an almost seventeen-year-old girl might have a million adventures there?

A voice at the back of my skull asks: "Just what kind of adventures are you looking for, Trisha?"

And I honestly don't know the answer.

Especially when I'm already happily going steady with Matt, smooth-sailing, easygoing, fun-arguing Matt, only sometimes maybe a little disturbing the way he makes my body react in a way I don't think I want.

Paul Newman rubs his tail across my cheek. "Don't worry, I'll feed you," I tell him.

There's a knock. Mom whips in wearing her classy black office dress and sipping a last-minute cup of coffee. "Zip me, sweetheart, will you?"

She smells of Chanel and instant espresso and Crest.

"I'm leaving scrambled eggs on the stove for you. Have a great trip, and don't forget to call me when you get there."

She kisses me quickly and she's gone. How come I never get around to asking her some of the questions that matter?

Like doesn't she ever get bored waking up in the same house, going to the same job, seeing the same people, day after day after day? Like doesn't she ever feel sometimes that people look so vacant?

Maybe I'm just suffering from senior class senility. If it weren't for this trip to New York, I'd be ready for a nursing home. Early retirement on my seventeenth birthday three months from now.

Sometimes it seems as if all of us—me, Matt, my girlfriends Toni and Ruth, probably even my worst enemy, that big beautiful Viking Nadine, who'd *love* to steal Matt from me—are stuck worrying about the future, as if what happens after graduation might be like getting trapped in a computer with no hope of getting out.

But today is different!

The downstairs door slams. The car catches and coughs. I fling myself to the window and throw it open.

"Mom! I love you!"

She can't hear me. Her car shoots out the driveway and down the street. The story of my life: Just when I yell, "I love you"—no one hears me.

Last night Mom's eyes were big and liquid when she said, "Be careful. It's not the safest place in the world."

"I know."

"Do you?"

She looked at me as if we were a thousand miles away from each other.

"I keep forgetting."

"What?"

"You're not thirteen anymore."

"I won't be wandering the streets alone, Mom."

How could I tell her what it feels like to be on my way to a classy hotel room near fabulous Fifth Avenue, with a collection of my best drawings and designs just in case some bigshot New York friend of Ms. Garfield wants to see what I can do?

"Excited?"

I nodded and suddenly hugged her very tight, as if I were afraid I'd lose her.

"Hey, you're not going to Mars. It's only Manhattan, Trisha."

Mom had been there for a couple of days on her honeymoon with Dad. How could she say *only* Manhattan? Because, dear Trisha, New York City is one big publicity trip designed to make the rest of America feel like it's Snoresville.

In reality, maybe the whole world is Snoresville and nobody is willing to admit it.

I'm still looking out the window, even though Mom's gone. Dad left before I got up, but last night he gave me a kiss and fifty dollars. "Mad money." He winked.

Inhaling the April-in-Cleveland smell of suburban

grass, I wonder if Matt loves me. Or me him. Maybe we'll fall in love in New York. We've been going together two years and it feels good and I think I sort of love him, but I haven't ever felt like I really *fell in love* with him—falling like a ton of bricks, I mean.

The only problem is, I don't like the way I feel when sometimes he gets me all shook up kissing. It's like I'm suspicious because he likes to hold me and kiss me and see my feelings get all stirred up until I have to break away. I don't like him liking that, and I almost don't like him being so attractive to me, because I still kind of feel there's a sort of magic or mystery that's missing.

A plunging hot shower steams up the bathroom. I'm sloughing off about a quarter-million dead cells from my body with the loofah, and halfway through my shower I'm suddenly dripping my way across the rug to the phone.

"Trisha, I can't go!"

It's my girlfriend Ruth's voice.

"Why?"

"My hair. I hate my hair. My hair is boring. It looks awful!"

"Ruth, I'll see you at the bus. We haven't got time to hate your hair. I'll fix your hair on the bus. I promise your hair won't be boring."

Ruth's voice perks up. "Will you really? Oh, Trish, I'm sorry I'm such a drag!"

"You're not a drag, Ruth."

"I'm a nerd, Trisha."

"You're definitely not a nerd. Herman is crazy about you."

"Herman Katzenellenbogen is crazy about a nerd!" She laughs. "Know what my horoscope says? Listen to this: 'Don't be afraid of sudden changes in your love life and creative challenges in your career. Ultimately, they'll benefit you.'"

When Ruth hangs up, her horoscope keeps echoing.

Sudden changes in your love life—does that mean Matt is going to propose to me? And your career, creative challenges . . . what career, I haven't even graduated high school! Don't kid yourself, Trisha, you'd love a career! You just don't have the guts to take it seriously.

Who says I don't have the guts? It's just that I forgot which bag I packed them in. Anyway it's *her* horoscope, not mine. And I did apply to a couple of colleges and art schools and got accepted. I'm just not sure which to go to. Am I sorry I didn't apply to a school in New York City?

I'm dripping my way back across the now-moist lavender shag rug to the still-running shower when the phone rings a second time.

"Trisha, do you wear regular or petite in pantyhose?"

"Toni, I don't have time! Matt's due here any minute and I'm still in the shower!"

"Then why did you answer the phone?" Toni asks in that calm, logical way of hers.

"Probably because my IQ is about minus eighty-four."

"Trisha, your sense of humor is what makes you a truly great personality."

"Sure, whenever I walk into an empty room, I always blend right in."

"May I return to the subject of pantyhose?" Toni continues her district attorney bit. "I forgot to buy extra pantyhose and I know I'll get a run in the ones I'm wearing on the bus and I do not want to step off the bus my first time in New York with my legs looking like I've been crawling through barbed wire. Can you lend me a pair of regular or not?"

"How can you change on the bus?"

"Has it occurred to you, my dear pal, that buses these days are often equipped with a bathroom?"

Toni and I have been friends since first grade. We always argue, but she and Ruth and I are *inseparable*.

So of course I'll lend her some pantyhose.

I almost reach the door to the bathroom, steam from the shower billowing out the opening, when the instrument of torture called the telephone does it again.

Is there a sixteen-year-old girl in America who can hear a phone ringing and not answer it?

"Trisha, it's me, Matt!"

Sometimes his voice sounds so grownup. Under my ribs there's an odd twinge. As if I suddenly realize he's not a boy. He's a man. Weird. Does a twinge under the ribs mean you're falling in love?

"My car broke down."

"Can't you take a cab, Matt? We'll miss the bus."

"Tow truck is on its way. I'll make it."

"What are you wearing, Matt?"

"What am I wearing? What do you mean, what am I wearing?"

"If I'm going to appear for the first time in my life on the streets of Manhattan with you, I want to wear something that matches what you're wearing."

"Well, I'm wearing something that really stops traffic—a 1971 Dodge Dart with a slant-six engine and a busted radiator.

"What are you doing anyway? I hear this strange noise in the background."

"I'm taking a shower."

"Hot or cold?"

"Peach."

"That's not a temperature."

"Colors have temperature."

"Trisha, you're not normal."

"My thermometer says ninety-eight point six and I'm going to hang up right now and pray that Ms. Garfield can talk the bus driver into waiting for you."

Slam phone down and shift into high gear, bouncing around the house like a human ping-pong ball. Brush okay white teeth; brush fairly wavy, chestnut hair; make a nice face nicer with light moisturizer and translucent powder and pink blush and blue eye pencil and mascara and pink mauve lips; splash on Cinnabar body lotion; yank into stunning black cashmere sweater, comfortable wine pull-on pants, ballerina-style flats; drag green suitcases to front door; telephone Dial-A-Cab; brush hair again; check tartan plaid tote bag for toothbrush, underarm deodorant stick, extra pantyhose for Toni, sketch pad and pencils and pens, makeup mirror and kit, sunglasses, new telescoping umbrella, new candy-striped bikini (in case the hotel has an indoor pool, which I forgot to ask Ms. Garfield), and then call Dad at his office to say goodbye again.

"You show those New York flash-in-the-pans we've got some style of our own out here in Ohio!"

Style. That's a word Ms. Garfield has been hammering into us all year. Anybody can have taste, but very few people have style.

The taxi honks outside. I'm switching my shoes to the shiny pumps and then back again to the flats, taking a last-minute look at my hair, which absolutely looks gunky. Last-minute foot powder in my shoes. I love my feet, especially my toes. The cab driver honks again. I'm out the door, green suitcases destroying my hands. A flash of fantasy hits me—the Charlie Chaplin boy breaking off a hunk of the Statue of Liberty and offering me a bite.

I'd like to tell Matt about the Charlie Chaplin boy, but I'm not sure why I'd be telling him, and it might make him jealous, which I think is rotten when you're going steady. Or he just might laugh at it, which would make me feel like killing him.

I'm so much into my own head I hardly glance at the taxi driver. He's wrestling my bags into the trunk of his cab when I suddenly yell, "Wait! I forgot to feed Paul Newman!"

"Paul Newman?" the taxi driver grunts. "You gotta feed Paul Newman?"

As I race back toward the front door, I hear his loud growly voice sounding like somebody has stapled his nose to his shoulders. "Paul Newman. Sure. Well, why not? The guy's got to eat somewhere!"

2

PATRICK HENRY, STUCK over the high school entrance, has a chipped nose. The building is prehistoric and most of the teachers—except for Ms. Garfield—are real dinosaurs.

My cab squeaks to a stop. I'm so excited I hardly glance at the cabbie as he dumps my luggage on the sidewalk. I drop some money into his outstretched palm and hear him with half an ear as he drives away: "For a friend of Paul Newman, can you spare it?"

I really don't have time to bother with cab drivers.

Milling around the entrance of Patrick Henry High are about twenty art and design or fashion merchandising seniors; suitcases and shoulderbags are scattered in an obstacle course around them. They're wearing everything from cropped jeans to dirndl skirts, bomber jackets to Edwardian vests, spike heels, loafers, cowboy boots, ballet slippers, you name it. And enough different kinds of perfume to have your nose arrested for drunken driving. You can imagine how many piggy banks got assassinated in the weeks before this trip.

Well, why not? Who knows, maybe Someone Big will see us pouring out sketches on our drawing pads along Broadway or in Greenwich Village and will whip out his card and say, "Come see me for a job when you graduate." Dream on, Trisha!

But there is an electricity in the babble of kids' voices that I've never heard before. Maybe it's just the nervousness of twenty hicks from Cleveland trying to act real sophisticated so they won't stick out like worms in the Big Apple.

Actually, the kids on the trip are probably the least hick kids in Patrick Henry. Most of us will probably end up in Cleveland, but the idea of a New York career in art or fashion plays in your mind like a marquee displaying your name. Soon I'll have to choose between college in Cleveland with Matt, where it will take four years to get certified as an art teacher like Ms. Garfield, or art school in Dallas where my mother's brother teaches and can help me. Of course, New York is *the* place to go, but I guess I didn't apply to New York because I figured on staying near Matt, or if not, at least with a relative nearby, like in Dallas. In New York, I'd be all alone.

My eyes scan the crowd, all of them jabbering and turning toward Ms. Garfield, who is giving some last-minute instructions. For a moment, no one sees me.

There's no sign of Matt. Lord, don't let him miss the bus!

No sign of Nadine Jorgensen either, the beautiful blond icicle who has eyes for Matt. I wouldn't mind at all if *she* missed the bus.

There's Toni all wrapped up in conversation with Marcia Carter—whose aunt is coming along as a chaperone—and Matt's two Abbot and Costello buddies: Fat Jack Tolliver, who isn't fat but used to be, and Teddy Jackson, who wears his hair in a huge oily pompadour. Marcia adores Fat Jack. Toni despises Teddy. Fat Jack wouldn't care if Marcia walked off a cliff. Teddy has a thick hide; no matter how Toni snubs him, he sticks to her like flypaper.

Personally, I could do without both Fat Jack and Teddy. They really act so slick I can't stand it, especially the way Matt gets so macho when he's with them.

And there's Ruth with Herman Katzenellenbogen, listening to Ms. Garfield remind everybody that she expects a minimum of twenty sketches per day in our art notebooks as a record of our visual experiences on the trip.

Ms. Garfield finishes and hooks an arm in Marcia Carter's arm to talk to her. Ms. Garfield is an arm-in-arm type of person; I feel good seeing her. She's got real electric green eyes, and her hands are always dancing. She's wearing a three-piece pantsuit—a single-button cardigan jacket with slash pockets slung over a cowl-neck blouse—and she looks as if she just dropped ten years of age into the school incinerator.

Ruth and Herman are head to head, interested only in each other. Ruth is slender, with wide shoulders I envy, large breasts that embarrass her, tiny feet, oval face, black bangs, tiny ears, and she's wearing a sensational snow-white Mandarin jacket with an emerald velour tunic underneath. She's jabbing her finger at Herman like she's giving him orders.

Herman looks like he loves it. He's kind of a teenage Albert Einstein, short, with sandy hair and eyeglass lenses thick as icecubes.

"Trisha!" Toni sees me and flings herself in my direction. Toni has a sleek hourglass figure, a mite bulgy—the kind of bulges boys like and girls don't—and thick tawny hair, a dramatic narrow face, high cheekbones, plucked eyebrows, and earrings down to her shoelaces.

"Did you," Toni whispers, "bring the pantyhose?"

I grin, nod, sweep my eyes around the twos and threes of kids gabbling away. Still no Matt.

"Ten days of freedom from the Patrick Henry assemblyline!" Toni gushes and shakes her thick head of hair. Her face assumes a sudden grimness as she yanks open her handbag for me to see a small metal bullhorn attached to a white can. "Any mugger gets near me in New York, I press the button and it blasts his eardrums apart."

"No one's going to mug us, Toni."

"I like to be prepared. Wasn't Matt supposed to drive you here?"

"Car trouble. He'll be along."

"You don't mind if I hate you a little, Trish, for having a steady boyfriend like Matt on your first trip to Manhattan."

"Just hate me nicely."

"I don't see Nadine. Wouldn't it be wonderful if she got sick or something?"

Nadine is like our mortal enemy in general, and mine in particular, partly because she acts as if she's Marie Antoinette, and partly because she goes on splashing her gorgeous Scandinavian everything in Matt's direction even though she knows he and I have a steady thing. In our considered opinion—me, Toni, Ruth—Nadine has a heart probably about the size and tenderness of a frozen pea.

A clapping of hands catches our attention. It's Ms. Garfield and Marcia's aunt, Miss Carter, getting the crowd of kids organized because a slick silver bus with tinted polarized windows has just swung around the corner toward Patrick Henry. Ms. Garfield zigzags through the mess of students, and I'm a little surprised she only nods at me. I'm usually her favorite, but maybe it's because she's nervous like the rest of us.

The bus jumps to a stop facing Patrick Henry's chipped nose. Where are you, Matt? Suppose he doesn't make it? My mind splits into equal halves—one half says it would be horrible not to share New York with him, while the other half says maybe a little distance from Matt would help, because when I see him every day the way I do, I can't think straight about whether I should do something adventurous all by myself after graduation or whether I should stay in Cleveland and keep dating Matt. And probably marry him.

Ruth breaks away from Herman and makes a beeline for me. "Trisha, how long have you been here?"

"Ruth, you look great!" I hug her.

Ruth shrinks a little when you hug her, but I always try anyway.

"I didn't know you had a Mandarin jacket, Ruth," Toni says in that trying-hard-to-be-friendly voice she uses with her.

Ruth glances back at Herman, who seems satisfied standing alone, and returns nice for nice as always with Toni. "I wish I could wear earrings the way you do."

Then, to me, Ruth whispers, "And don't forget you promised to do my hair. Herman likes it the way it is, but he has no taste in hair."

I guess the only reason Ruth and Toni have stayed friends all through junior high and high school is because they like me enough to put up with each other.

Anyway, pretty soon the whole gang of us avalanche into the bus. The driver has a bald watermelon head which he keeps shining nervously with the palm of his hand as he watches us, a dubious look on his face. I swear he must be praying, "Help me survive a ride to New York with this gang of overdressed rinkydinks without kicking at least one of them in the butt!"

Soon the bus is filled, except for two vacant seats, one next to me for Matt, and one next to Ms. Garfield for Nadine. I forgot to mention that Nadine and I are probably her two best art students.

The busdriver swipes his palm across the top of his head, then eyeballs his wristwatch for the hundredth time, grinds his teeth, and grumbles to himself.

"You think Matt will make it?" Ruth asks me, worried. She is worried because she thinks Matt and I are perfect for each other.

I don't answer her. Ruth pats my hand. Playing mommy comes naturally to her. She glances out the window at Herman, who is standing on the sidewalk with a very heavy smile on his face.

"Listen, lady," the driver complains to Ms. Garfield, "I got my orders what time to leave. This here bus has got to get going. Those two kids don't make it, nothing I can do."

Ms. Garfield gets an inspiration. "Just let me make one sketch of your face. You see, this is an art class, and your face is really unique."

She begins sketching the busdriver with swift slashes of her pen, and he can't resist falling into a pose. "Don't make my ears too big, lady. Five more minutes, then we gotta go."

In exactly five minutes Ms. Garfield hands the driver a sketch of his face which I think is sensational. He shakes his head gloomily. "You got a little talent there, lady."

The engine of the bus kicks into action.

Sympathetically, from across the aisle, Ms. Garfield slides her bright green eyes into touch with mine. "Any ideas about Matt?"

"Just that his car broke down."

The bus lurches forward. Patrick Henry and Herman Katzenellenbogen disappear behind us in a gust of exhaust.

Ms. Garfield glances at me as if she expects me to commit hara kiri without Matt. I smile back weakly. How do you explain that just two weeks ago, I couldn't *live* if Matt didn't call me twice a day, but now that he's actually missed the bus, I feel scared, as if, without Matt, I'll have to play a whole different part in New York. It might be even more thrilling on my own, which is why I feel kind of guilty that I'm not as disappointed as I should be that he's not here.

Maybe it has something to do with my recent dreams about the Charlie Chaplin boy.

The sound of a car horn evaporates the image of those dreams from my thoughts, and I see a yellow Volkswagen racing alongside the bus, an older woman at the steering wheel and Nadine Jorgensen and Matt waving and yelling at the busdriver to stop.

One of the reasons it's so easy to hate Nadine is that she has a gorgeous waterfall of platinum blond hair, a gorgeous tall Raquel Welch body, gorgeous straight nose, gorgeous Viking blue eyes—gorgeous everything.

I have to admit that seeing Matt with her makes me much more sensitive to his warm brown eyes, curly black hair, the strong planes of his face, the presence of his muscular slim-hipped body.

Minutes later the two of them are seated—Matt with me, Nadine next to Ms. Garfield—and the busdriver, with a questioning look to heaven, rams the bus into gear.

"Glad to see me?" Matt asks softly.

"Of course." I'm also using a low breathy voice, because I don't want Nadine—who is busy being gorgeous in her seat at the window, separated from us only by Ms. Garfield and the aisle—to eavesdrop on Matt and me.

"You don't *sound* glad." Matt has a way of cuddling his words sometimes that could melt an iceberg. I love his wonderfully glossy hair and his eyes and the curve of his jaw.

"I was thinking of a boy who looks like Charlie Chaplin."

"Do I know him?"

"I doubt it."

"Where'd you meet him?"

"I've only seen him a few times."

"Am I supposed to be jealous?"

"Yes."

"I'm not."

"You should be. He's very attractive. He awakens all my savage instincts."

Matt grins, his eyes like magnets. Sometimes I resent how easy it is for him to make me feel like melted Velveeta.

"Does he go to Patrick Henry?"

"Will you admit that you're a little bit jealous?"

"You want me to be jealous of a guy I've never met?"

"Yes."

"You're from outer space, Trisha!"

"So are you."

"Name one thing that makes me spacey!"

"You call and tell me your car is broken down, and then you arrive here with Nadine Jorgensen."

"I did not arrive *with* Nadine. I arrived and Nadine arrived."

"In the same car."

"She was on her way to catch the bus and passed me just when the tow truck got my car hooked up to take to the garage."

"I bet she was parked around the corner from your house on a stake-out all night, just waiting to follow you. I bet she sabotaged your engine by pouring Chanel Number Five into the carburetor."

"Trisha, Nadine and I are just good friends. We've known each other since kindergarten."

"Her brain may be in kindergarten but her body has a full-tuition scholarship to college!"

Matt laughs and squeezes my hand. He touches my chin with his fingertips.

"You're supposed to be angrily demanding to know the name of the boy who looks like Charlie Chaplin."

"I don't want to know his name because I might just bust his jaw."

"That's more like it. Anyway, he's someone I don't know but I keep dreaming about him."

"Well, I don't mind what you do with him if you're asleep, but just don't dream about him when you're awake. Anyway, maybe he's really *me,* only your subconscious can't admit it to yourself."

We laugh together, relaxing and holding hands and listening to the buzz and chatter of our classmates, who sound like birds all singing different songs at the same time. Once in a while you can distinguish Toni's so-phisticated voice or Ruth's scratchy voice or the drippy voice of Miss Carter, the toothpick-thin volunteer chaperone aunt of Marcia Carter, or the occasional grunt from the busdriver.

Leaning back in the seat, my shoulder touching Matt's, our fingers laced together, watching the road east from Cleveland, I think I can see the whole future ahead of us: Matt and I graduating, working hard through college or art school, Matt in his dad's art publicity business in Cleveland, me doing graphics or fashion design or book illustration, the two of us getting married and setting up our own little apartment, having parties, loads of friends over for dinner, Toni, Ruth, maybe even Ms. Garfield. It looks really pretty happy, which is why it's peculiar that I feel so depressed.

After the first couple of hours on the bus, it begins to seem like musical chairs. Kids are switching seats all over the place, a dozen conversations going at once.

"I think it's the dumbest place I ever heard to have a senior prom in."

"And I think you ought to have it layer cut, like about chin-length, and then curl it with a curling iron and brush it back."

"Sure, they've got a great batting lineup, but where's their pitching?"

"Better bring a vacuum cleaner, I hear New York is pretty dirty. Ha-ha."

"It's only dirty if you have a dirty mind!"

"You know, you've got the IQ of a dead ant!"

Matt and Fat Jack and Teddy are squeezed into the back seat in a blistering argument about batting averages and which team will do what to whom and how. I keep bopping from one friend to another, all over the bus, but mostly with Ruth and Toni.

Toni, after she puts the pantyhose I brought for her, sinks into one of her hopeless moods. "I absolutely think human relationships between people are impossible, Trisha, especially with boys, but then I think maybe I should date an older guy, like twenty-two or -three maybe, only just my luck he'll ask me to marry him and then he'll get run over by a hit-and-run driver."

When I do Ruth's hair for her we have a nice conversation about Herman Katzenellenbogen. Ruth feels Herman definitely should not become a physics genius because she is absolutely sure he and she will be happier if he is a famous surgeon, since surgeons make more money than movie stars if you take into account the total number of years they can keep earning. I am envious of Ruth because she somehow makes Herman furiously happy by winding him tighter and tighter around her little finger, and I don't have the faintest idea how she does it. Every so often she digs into the box he gave her as a going-away present: love notes, chocolate-covered raisins, Band-aids, a plastic rose, peanut brittle, Lifesavers, cough drops, spearmint gum, magazines, extra pencils, a pencil sharpener—all keep testifying to Herman's adoration.

Ruth and Herman never seem to argue. They know who's boss. Matt and I don't know who's boss, and we have so many little storms between us.

Like I will say to Matt, "Did you see that rerun of *Love Boat* last night?"

And he will say, "*Love Boat* is baloney."

"I think it happens to be very funny and romantic."

"It's so phony."

Or he will ask me to watch two men in silk shorts

and boxing gloves trying to put each other in the hospital, and I'll say, "It should be against the law."

And he'll snap at me: "If two guys want to fight to make a living, would you rather put them on an unemployment line instead?"

"Maybe if we gave them an education, they could be terrific ballet dancers."

Maybe arguing is part of enjoying each other, except that the way we do it hurts, although we always get back to the good feelings. Even though getting back feels good, I think I'd rather we didn't argue.

Anyway, the worst moment of the bus ride is when I'm gabbing away with Marcia Carter, who *hates* that her aunt is a chaperone on the trip, and over my shoulder I see Nadine digging the fingers of both her hands into Matt's neck. He winks at me. My blood boils.

"You were busy talking," Matt explains to me later, when we are sitting elbow to elbow, "and I asked around for some aspirin for a headache and Nadine insisted on doing that massage business. I'm not kidding, Trisha. My head is really killing me!"

So I go around asking for aspirin for Matt and, naturally, from somewhere in the jumble of goodies in Ruth's gift box she nips out a bottle of aspirin.

"Want to know your astrological advice for today?" Ruth asks.

You can't say no without offending Ruth's feelings, so I nod my head dutifully.

"You're a Leo...listen to this, Trisha! 'Play your cards carefully. Today's activities could have a profound effect on your career. A romance you thought headed for the rocks can still be salvaged.'"

"Thanks, Ruth."

Sympathy is practically dripping out of her eyes. "Are you and Matt headed for the rocks?"

"We're planning never to see each other again and then get married."

Ruth's face looks hurt.

"I'm sorry, Ruth."

She perks up and offers me two jagged hunks of Herman's peanut brittle. "Give a piece to Matt," she advises in her motherly way.

Then we lean back into our seats and watch the bus window framing a stream of clouds, meadows, ridged hills, the round April sun. I find myself thinking about Ms. Garfield, because the most peculiar part of the trip, as far as I am concerned, is the mood Ms. Garfield drifted into the moment we left Cleveland. Her dancing hands and eyes stopped dancing, and I noticed how she kept unfolding a beige envelope and reading and rereading the letter inside, pursing her mouth intently as we went rushing through the Ohio countryside. Now I see her staring through the window as the bus cuts along the Pennsylvania Turnpike, staring as if her life depended on it at the ragged evergreen trees and the outcropping of gray rocks.

And then, finally, hours later, we're coming off the Jersey Turnpike. Near the Hudson River, I see the Statue of Liberty looking sort of small and green on a thumbnail island in New York Harbor. Skyscrapers rising out of Manhattan like silver spears. The Hudson River bouncing pieces of sunlight off its waves. And ferryboats, just like my dream. My heart feels like a balloon about to explode. Everybody is trying to act sophisticated, but I can tell they'd like to squash their noses against the tinted bus windows.

"This is it, folks," Ms. Garfield announces, and I hear a definite quiver to her voice, "a short ride under the river."

Our bus roars into a tunnel, two lanes heading east under the Hudson River, and then out into the light.

Manhattan. Spotless, definitely not. Sweet-smelling, you can't say so. Welcoming, not on your life. Metal and glass and stone, and faces that, at first, look too busy to stop for anything less than an earthquake.

But you feel something special in the streets, in the traffic, in the people and lights and buildings. Like anything can happen, even to a high school senior from Cleveland.

Our driver groans at the crazy and impolite taxis that cut in front of us. Even from the bus windows, you feel the enormous size of the city, the pulse of people on the crowded sidewalks. You ask yourself, what do I want here? A thrill? Something extraordinary? To get away from my boring, conventional self? A new perspective?

Any minute we're expecting to see the beautiful, modern, reasonably priced Hotel Manhattan (so said the brochures) awaiting us with swift elevators, hot showers, luxurious mattresses and breathtaking views.

The bus inches down Fifth Avenue, one-way traffic so jammed together you wish you had eyes on every side of your head because the crowds of people are a show in themselves—every race and size and shape, rich, poor, old, young, peddlers hawking hot dogs and orange juice and fruit and jewelry and sweaters, a policeman writing a ticket, a truck driver shaking his fist at a cab driver, horns, brakes, engines, construction, yelling, running whistles—noise and speed and rhythm.

Our bus gets caught at a red light on Fifth Avenue, ready for a right turn down Thirty-first Street. A woman in dark brown pants and a coffee-with-cream tunic is blasting her police whistle and whipping her arm to manipulate traffic. And there, not twenty yards from the bus, is my Charlie Chaplin boy.

Yes, the boy who's been haunting my dreams.

I see him there on the sidewalk in front of a glass and aluminum office building that rises up so slick and sleek that there doesn't seem to be a top to it.

Of course he doesn't look anything like Charlie Chaplin, but I *know*, beyond a shadow of a doubt. Every atom of my instinct says this is him.

A shiver of fear and wonder runs through my body, as if I were entering a fairy tale where startling and wonderful things could happen... and you might never find your way back.

The boy is tall, a head taller than I dreamed him, but shorter than Matt. He's wearing a tight black t-shirt, black dancer's pants and floppy black boots; a stiff, black, curve-brimmed hat perches on the back of his head; his hair is long and wavy gold with sparks of red. Maybe I can't really *see* the sparks of red at this distance but I *feel* them. There's a gold earring in his right earlobe. He has thick eyebrows. His eyes are hypnotic, intensified by the white greasepaint covering all the rest of his face. People—half a dozen pedestrians—have stopped to watch him.

On the sidewalk at his feet there's a black box, apparently for contributions because a green bill and some silver peek out.

Is he a mime? A dancer? No, a magician! Colored scarves appear in his hands. He grins. The scarves vanish. He scowls. They reappear. The scarves change color. His eyes seem to be so melancholy when the scarves disappear, and so delighted when he plucks them out of the air.

Then the traffic light blinks green. The busdriver sighs loudly and swings the steering wheel. I see the boy magician pretending to weep. His street audience laughs. Wait! Wait for me! I've got to speak to him!

The bus rolls halfway down the block and jerks to a stop in front of the HO EL MAN A TAN. I'm the first one out the door and I'm racing back toward the center of Fifth Avenue. It's crazy. It's only a silly dream. He doesn't look one bit like my Charlie Chaplin dream boy. But I have to—*have to*—see him.

3

THEY'RE ALL SO busy grabbing handbags, brushing crumbs off their clothes, slinging their arms through the straps of shoulderbags, I doubt if anyone on the bus sees me weaving along the sidewalk through a horde of grinning Japanese businessmen, at least thirty of them, each wearing identical blue blazers with a gold logo on the breast pocket. Then I'm around the corner.

Yes, he is there.

He sinks his teeth into a huge red apple and then flips it up into the air. Then another apple and another and another. Laughter flickers through the sidewalk audience. The apples whirl around him as if they have a power of their own and his hands are merely platforms for taking off.

Does he notice me in the fringe of onlookers? His eyes—gray-blue eyes full of secrets and surprises—flash past me. I wonder what he sees in my face. Am I wearing the kind of smile he likes?

Now a scissor in his deft fingers begins to snip at a rope, and snip and snip, until he flings the rope up into the air like a chopped snake, and the audience applauds because the snipped pieces of rope are all one piece again.

Suddenly he dashes like a ballet dancer into the traffic, cars braking inches from him, and he reaches toward the clouds, catching hold of an invisible rope from the sky, which he hauls down, hand over hand, red-faced and sweating, huffing and puffing, with humble apologetic looks at the halted cars, while horns honk angrily and people giggle.

His limbs and torso seem absolutely boneless as he hops back onto the sidewalk and begins to pantomime a fisherman unable to catch anything in the sea of traffic, until a powerful creature gets hooked on his line and nearly drowns him. Then he becomes a waiter piling dishes and glasses on a tray until he can hardly lift it, and stumbling under the weight of the tray he falls flat on his backside.

It is his silence that clings to me. His lips and eyes and eyebrows are so mobile, and his fingers shape the air into fascinating forms. His face, painted so starkly white, terrified, or fierce with rage or poetic with suffering, seems to promise a world of imagination and mysteries.

At last he bows to the audience, dropping from the waist like a rag doll, and his legs crumple under him. The audience, beginning to drift away, gives him a scattering of handclaps. He flips off his hard black hat so that it sails up and around and down into the palm of his hand, and he holds out the hat for contributions, his eyes glinting mischievously, framed by his thatch of flaming hair.

An elegant white-haired man drops a coin into the black hat. A frilly girl with upswept hair drops a coin. A young square-jawed executive drops a coin. A girl of six, pushed forward by her mother, drops a coin. The coins clink against each other in the black hat, not much at all. The audience dissolves except for me. But the boy doesn't appear to see me. He shrugs, shakes the few coins out of the hat, and shoves them into his pocket. For the first time I notice the hollowness of his cheeks, and I wonder if he gets enough to eat.

I tap him on the shoulder as he gathers his magic gear together. Half turning, he cocks one eye at me over his shoulder. I'm holding out a dollar bill. With a look of ferocious concentration, he transforms his left hand into an airplane doing spins and dives and loops, swooping toward the dollar and snatching it away between his fingers.

"I enjoyed your act."

"Can I call you Pocahantas?"

Is it just mischievousness in his voice that makes me feel as if he's inviting me someplace I've never been?

His eyes smile into mine and he says, "Agent X4Z calling HQ. Come in, HQ! The message for tonight is: A journey to the moon for the blue mouse. Repeat: A journey to the moon for the blue mouse."

The two of us stand there staring at each other, while people pour around us like water over two rocks in a river.

I know he is waiting for me to say something.

Never in my entire life have I felt so peculiar, looking without any walls or fences or protection or the slightest embarrassment into the gray-blue eyes of a boy. It's as if we knew each other in some other life a thousand years ago and we need no words because there are no barriers at all between us.

I feel as if we are putting down roots through the cracks in the sidewalk—sort of—both of us reaching into each other with our eyes, until the sound of a loud horn honking suddenly reminds me of my classmates and Ms. Garfield and Matt.

I take a step away from him, but he touches my arm

and miraculously a white card appears in his fingers. The card passes from him to me: It reads:

Vic Uris
Magic and Mime
226-1191

I am racing away from Fifth Avenue, toward the HO EL MAN A TAN. The white card clutched in my fist feels like a talisman, and the words keep repeating inside me: "A journey to the moon for the blue mouse."

4

VIC URIS IS behind me. I know he won't be standing there if I turn around, so I don't turn around, even though every molecule says, "Turn around, Trisha, it might be the last time you ever see him."

Every step away from him and back toward the bus is like tearing myself free from some unknown danger. Why do I sense danger? A danger to him or to me? Is it because of my dream?

But I know he's not really the Charlie Chaplin boy. Dreams are dreams and reality is reality. It's all the effect of arriving in New York and knowing that someday this might be where I'll make my life—where the art is, where the fashion is, where the excitement is. If I don't marry Matt.

And what makes me so sure Matt will ever ask me?

Up ahead, in front of the canopy where the electric lights spell out HO EL MAN A TAN, Ms. Garfield is in the midst of two dozen yakking students, dancing her hands like an orchestra conductor trying to bring harmony out of chaos, suitcases and duffel bags strewn underfoot. The gleaming silver bus jerks away from the sidewalk. My handbag! I'm sure Matt took my suitcases off, but my handbag—my handbag is on the bus under my seat!

I sprint into the gutter, dodging a delivery van. Racing past the hotel entrance, I catch a jumble of views like snapshots flung at my eyes: Ms. Garfield pointing her finger at me, the volunteer chaperone Miss Carter holding her forehead between two fingers like pincers as if she were about to lose her lunch, Matt and Nadine chatting in a sophisticated pose on the red-carpeted hotel steps, Toni sketching a drunk asleep on the sidewalk, Ruth dipping into Herman's gift box for a marshmallow to remind her of his humble, undying affection.

"Stop!" I shout at the bus as it coughs exhaust fumes in my face.

"Trisha, wait!" Matt calls from behind me.

What amazes me is that obviously only minutes have passed since the bus arrived—a handful of minutes that I spent watching Vic Uris do his act—yet to me the special world Vic created was a world without clocks or minutes or hours, a world where a century happens in seconds.

I catch up to the bus at a stoplight and bang on the front door. The door folds open. The busdriver's eyes, I notice for the first time, are a pleasant shade of blue.

"Please, I left my handbag under my seat."

"Sure, take your time." The driver seems so much more relaxed and friendly now, pointing his thumb toward the back of the bus.

I climb inside. I crane my neck under my seat. My handbag is nowhere in sight. All I find are balled-up chewing gum wrappers and candy wrappers and the wrinkled beige envelope with the letter I saw Ms. Garfield reading. I stuff the letter into the pocket of my cardigan jacket, wondering if I'll read it before I give it back to Ms. Garfield.

Horns are squawking behind the bus. "Sorry you couldn't find it," the driver says gruffly. "Look, you call

your folks; they can send you money. You need a dime
for a phone call?"

I shake my head. "Thanks anyway."

Then I'm standing on the sidewalk. The driver waves,
the bus pulls away. I feel bad for the driver; he's got a
hard and tedious job. I also feel lost without my handbag.
But the card still crushed in my fist reminds me of magic,
of the secrets and surprises in someone's eyes. Did he
want me to phone him?

Funny how Vic Uris reminds me of stories my dad
and mom used to read me—stories about princesses and
witches, magic potions, enchanted swans, how a kiss
transforms a frog into a prince.

Somebody taps me on the shoulder. I turn and see my
handbag a foot from my face, and on the other end of
the handbag is Matt. I feel like I've been cast in concrete.
Gently, he lays the strap of the handbag over my shoulder. The concrete turns to jelly.

"Thanks, Matt."

"I thought you decided to jog back to Cleveland."

"Without you?"

"What's happening, Trisha?"

"About what?"

"I've noticed lately that sometimes we'll be walking
along or doing some normal thing and suddenly without
warning you're a million miles away."

"A million miles? No wonder my feet hurt."

"You'll never win a victory if you think about *de-
feat*!"

"I guess I seem different because of the class trip.
The closer we came to the trip, the more scared I got."

"There's nothing to be scared of, Trisha!"

"Maybe I'm scared because the closer we came to
this trip, the more I began to think that I should have
applied to an art school in New York. It's the place to
make a career in art, except that it would be so far away

from you—I don't think I have the guts to come here alone."

Matt's face moves within kissing distance. "I didn't even want you to apply to Dallas."

"My parents thought I should."

"You can have a career in Cleveland, Trisha. I think you're going to stay in Cleveland."

"What if I don't want to?"

"I'll rent a small apartment and chain you to the stove."

His long downswept eyelashes send a quiver of excitement through me. "Is that all you want, Matt, someone to cook for you?"

"No! I have to have someone to argue with, too!"

For a moment his eyes are so dark and serious, looking sort of inward, but he shakes off the mood quickly. "I bet there isn't a nose in New York City that wrinkles like yours."

I laugh in spite of myself. "What about Nadine's nose?"

"She has one of those drip-dry noses, never wrinkles."

He takes my hand and wheels me around toward the HO EL MAN A TAN. "Just don't go around wrinkling your nose at anybody but me."

His voice is playful, but I catch a flash of hardness in his eyes.

5

IN THE FIFTEEN years since Ms. Garfield last lived in the Big Apple, HO EL MAN A TAN has obviously gone downhill, even though its advertising brochure still makes it appear glamorous. Downhill means rain and pollution have made the face of the hotel look like its mascara is running, and knots of seedy characters are hanging around the hotel entrance. Downhill means no doorman, worn carpets, a smell of disinfectant, a bellhop with a broken nose slouching and smirking and not offering to help with our bags. Downhill means that the hotel has one less room than we reserved, and that the elevator is out of order.

In the hotel lobby a pair of hands is doing a war dance. The hands belong to Ms. Garfield. The object of her war dance is a square-faced man with jowls down to his lapels and a tilted toupee.

"Believe me, Miss Garfinkle—"

"Garfield! *Ms*. Garfield!"

"Of course. As I was trying to explain, it is the policy of the Hotel Manhattan, of which I have been assistant manager for a total of twelve years, to provide decent accommodations for people from all over the world, including Cleveland—"

"All I want to know is why my students do not have the number of rooms we were promised."

Listening, I am reminded of the letter I found that belongs to Ms. Garfield, but that gets forgotten as Ms. Garfield throws up her hands in despair—there's no chance of getting another room for us because the hotel is booked tight.

So we grit our teeth and start hauling suitcases up six and seven flights of stairs. I don't recommend it. Especially when Amazon Nadine strides past you holding her bags as if they were feathers, without even getting out of breath.

"Hating Nadine makes it all worthwhile," I offer cheerfully to Toni, whose knees are buckling as she strains at the handles of her overstuffed suitcases.

"Care for a coughdrop?" Ruth asks, puffing.

I shake my head, wondering where Matt is—he went bounding up the stairs with Fat Jack and Teddy, and Nadine was bounding right after them.

"Did you *see* those people in the lobby?" Toni croaks.

"I thought they looked interesting," Ruth says mildly. "How about a Lifesaver?"

"You look at their eyes," Toni hissed.

"I have lemon and cherry and—"

"Ruth!" Toni erupts.

"Toni," I intervene before an argument flares, "if we all stay together, no one will bother us."

With a peacemaking gesture, Ruth says, "Toni, I've got the kind of licorice you like."

"This city is full of nuts ready to grab your jewelry and knock you down. You planning to defend yourself with licorice and Lifesavers?"

The long ragged line of Patrick Henry seniors and Ms. Garfield and poor Miss Carter extends from the lobby and up along the staircase to the sixth and seventh floors. When we finally drag our feet at last into room 703—

Toni, Ruth and I—we find Nadine testing one of the beds.

"Ms. Garfield," Nadine explains in that deep maple-syrup voice of hers, "put me in here because we have one less room."

"Oh, joy!" I exclaim.

"Do you realize," Toni warns us all darkly, "that we are the only high school students on the seventh floor?"

I pat Toni's shoulder. "We'll survive."

It isn't until I finally have my turn in the bathroom that I look again at the white card that Vic Uris had pressed into my hand. His phone number catches at my eyes.

I force my thoughts away from Vic Uris and concentrate on Ms. Garfield's letter. You have no right to read it, Trisha. Just return it. Ms. Garfield has been kind of an important person to me for the past two years. The only adult I really wanted to be like, a role model sort of, a big part of my desire to learn about art and design and fashion. She deserves your respect and you shouldn't read her mail. You hear me, Trisha?

The letter is brief:

Dear Tracy,

Fifteen years is a long time without any word from the girl who turned down my first and last marriage proposal ever. I've been painting pieces of you on canvas ever since, in one form or another. Even when I paint a bowl of apples or a mytho-logical lion or a bigmouth politician, you are there. Of course I'd be delighted to show my studio to your students and speak to them. But I'd be even more delighted if you and I can warm a few mem-ories together. This time I can even afford to take you to dinner. Remember that restaurant in

Chinatown, across the street from the statue of Confucius?

Still waiting,
Jack

An hour later, when we are all spiffed up in our most glamorous outfits and on our way to our first dinner in Manhattan, I hand the crumpled letter to Ms. Garfield.

"Found it on the bus when I was searching the floor for my handbag."

"Thank you, Trisha."

She takes my arm. We've been walking from our hotel. Ms. Garfield refuses to take a bus or train, since the April weather is balmy and she wants us to get the feel of Manhattan. The sky is all cotton candy, pink and mauve, reflecting the lights everywhere and especially the colored floodlights on the tower of the Empire State Building. Darkness sort of settles over the city like a black cloak over the shoulders of a beautiful woman wearing more diamonds than you can count.

"Did you read the letter, Trisha?"

"No."

"I would have, if I had been you."

"Well, I—I did read it."

"I'm glad."

"Why, Ms. Garfield?"

"It's nice to have someone on the trip who knows a little about me as a human being. Someone who won't spread gossip—I hope. It's a lot less lonely."

"I shouldn't have read your letter. I'm really sorry."

"I wasn't much older than you when I met Jack Malamud right here in Manhattan. He was painting and starving, and he wanted me to marry him."

"Did you love him?"

"Not enough to be poor. I met a handsome cheerful successful lawyer from Cleveland and he and Cleveland made me quite happy. We had no children but I loved teaching; the two of us went to parties, played tennis, had so many friends. He died of a heart attack a year before I met you, Trisha."

There was a painful silence.

"And now I guess I'm scared to see Jack Malamud again. Because I might find out that during all those years in Cleveland I was just fooling myself into thinking I was happy."

"He's a big name in painting, isn't he?"

She nodded. "You and I are much alike, Trisha."

"How?"

"I think we want life to be very, very intense, beautiful, not stale or repetitious, but we also want to play it safe. We hold back."

"I'm not sure I understand."

"Neither am I."

Loops of electric lights along the brick face of a building welcome us to Mamma Leone's restaurant.

But dinner isn't nearly as thrilling as I expected it to be, because I keep asking myself if Ms. Garfield is right about me. Do I hold back in my relationship with Matt, for example? Definitely. I glance across the table at him now—he's laughing and eating, and when his eyes meet mine they are terribly inviting. I can feel the force of his eyes as if he were holding me close to him. I can feel the hard swift way he always kisses me, and the force of his body against mine, the way his eyes radiate power—and the way I click shut at those moments.

What about a boy like Vic Uris, who seems so different from Matt, yet maybe they're all the same when they want something from you. I've hardly ever dated anyone but Matt. Would Vic Uris make me click shut too?

Matt winks at me across the plates of pasta. Where I hold back with him, I think, is when I sense that he wants me to be more than his steady girl—he wants me to say

I love him or that I belong to him and only him forever and ever.

But I can't. Not yet. He's wonderful and he puts my solar plexus on a roller coaster ride, but I don't know if that means I love him, and I don't want to tell Matt I love him and get him so awfully involved that he'll be badly hurt if we have to go our separate ways. Besides, *he's* never said he loves *me*.

Maybe that's why I slip away during dessert, and I plop into a phone booth and dial the number on the white card. But the moment the phone rings my courage goes down the drain. Just as well. I wouldn't have much time to see Vic Uris anyway. Our schedule is loaded for the next nine days.

When I get back to the table and dig my spoon into the tortoni, a sense of disappointment makes it harder for me to enjoy all the giggling and kidding and put-on sophistication.

Even though it's dark on the walk back to our hotel, I feel quite safe with so many of us sticking together.

"Watch out for pickpockets!" the word passes from mouth to ear to mouth.

Ms. Garfield's enthusiasm about sketching the nightlife is contagious, and she has us stop now and then to give our blank paper a workout. A number of kids, especially Toni, are constantly swinging their eyes around for fear of muggers. She's afraid of muggers, and I'm afraid of Vic Uris, for totally different reasons.

It's fascinating to watch the different people in our group reacting to the city; some of them are loosening up, others tightening.

Fat Jack Tolliver, with his bristly marine haircut, and slick Teddy Jackson, with his oily pompadour, seem to think New York is just the right place to be noisier and more annoying than usual, and they grab Matt away from me.

Ruth might as well be in Cleveland for all the difference it makes, as she chews the little gift candies from her box. Toni clings to my arm, tensely awaiting her first mugger. Nadine seems to be making points with Ms. Garfield.

The most dramatic reaction to Manhattan seems to be Miss Carter's: Our chaperone hasn't stopped sneezing since we left the hotel.

The broken-nosed bellboy, standing on a ladder, tapes together a rip in the canvas canopy and ignores us as we troop back into the hotel. Inside the lobby, I dart into a phone booth. Again I dial Vic Uris's number.

A boy's voice—it must be him—crackles into my ear.

"Welcome to the land of Vic Uris, king, prime minister, general of the army, director of the National Vic Uris Repertory Theater of Magic and Mime, chief construction engineer, plumber, electrician, head chef, caretaker, and population in general. When you hear the beep, please say something funny or inspiring, and leave your number so I can call you back, unless I owe you money."

His voice has that same strange quality, soft and full of shadows, as if he is leading you by the hand, gently, away from the everyday world and into . . . what?

The message I leave for him is: "Pocahantas here. I'm staying with my fellow high school seniors from Cleveland in the Hotel Manhattan. My number is 674-2313. You do not owe me money. P. S. The moon looks too far away for a blue mouse to get there."

As I leave the phone booth I spot Ms. Garfield in a booth nearby, and in the one next to her is Ruth, neither one aware of the other or of me. Ruth appears to be solemnly lecturing her beloved Herman while rotating a golfball of gum between her teeth and cheek. Ms. Garfield is laughing into the mouthpiece of her phone— laughing, but tears are raining down her cheeks.

I don't at all like seeing Ms. Garfield so shaky and

uncertain. Is she talking to Jack Malamud? I'm starting to dislike the man.

I guess I never realized how often it made me feel secure to see Ms. Garfield so perky and sure of herself in school or when she invited a bunch of us over to her apartment or took us to an art exhibit.

This worrying thought about Ms. Garfield keeps intruding as I climb the seven flights to our room. It keeps intruding along with visions of Vic Uris, his penetrating eyes, the dramas his hands and body create, and keeps intruding even as our first night in the hotel turns into a late-night pillow party, bunches of kids switching from room to room (even though we were warned not to), sitting on each other's beds and floors, surging with an energy that wags our tongues a mile a minute. It's partly the effect of being in New York in a somewhat suspicious hotel while the responsible adults are sleeping, as well as all our pent-up energy and the sense of being suddenly more grown up, seeing the shady and colorful characters around the hotel—the bellhop with suspicious eyes, the assistant hotel manager with the tilted toupee, the hard-eyed men and women in flashy clothes. It's as if the city, in a million different voices—and without the protective presence of our families—is yelling at us: "Hey, come on in and have a look around! Grab a piece of the action!"

At one point, 1:40 A. M., when the partying starts to fizzle, I find myself suddenly alone with Matt for a few minutes, and he takes my hand.

"I haven't kissed you since last week."

His voice sends the blood pounding in my veins. My fingers quiver, caught inside his huge hand.

"Do you like it when I kiss you, Trisha?"

I nod my head. I'd like to tell him how his nearness makes me tremble, and how I don't really understand why it makes me resent him just because he looks like he's enjoying it.

But I know if I tell him he'll misunderstand. He'll think I'm in love with him forever.

And how can I be in love with him forever when I find myself listening at the same time to a voice inside my head that says, "Can I call you Pocahantas?"

6

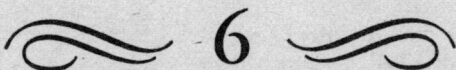

"WHY ARE YOU opening the window?"

"To look at the stars."

"Nadine, windows are made of glass so you can see through them without opening them up."

"I can't breathe with the window closed, Toni."

"You're going to leave the window open so some lunatic can climb in while we're all asleep?"

"You've already got a chair under the doorknob!"

"What good is having the door blocked if the window is wide open? We might as well put a sign up saying, 'Hey, you want to rob somebody, come right in!'"

"Well, I can't breathe without fresh air!"

"You won't breathe if someone climbs in here and slits our throats!"

I'm stretched across my bed, half listening to Toni and Nadine argue. Ruth has fallen asleep with her hair in curlers and a heart-shaped box of marzipan candies breathing up and down on her stomach. Without waking her, I remove the marzipan. I've never asked her how she can be so sure about her relationship with Herman.

"I've got a solution!" I interrupt. "I'll pick a number from one to ten, and whichever one of you gets it first decides the window."

Nadine picks eight, Toni picks two. Nadine picks ten, Toni picks six. I haven't picked a number, I just want to give them both the feeling that I'm honest. Nine, says Nadine; five, says Toni.

"Five it is!"

Toni closes the window.

Sure, I fixed the outcome, but I knew Nadine could sleep with the closed window and Toni would be a wreck with an open window.

A few minutes later I hear three sets of lungs breathing their individual rhythms. In the darkness the window seems like a porthole in a ship's cabin, as if the whole island of Manhattan is one enormous ocean liner gliding through silent jagged canyons.

I hope Vic Uris never calls.

I wish I could dial his number and erase the message I left for him.

Perhaps I could call and leave a second message: "Hi, this is Pocahantas again. Sorry, my plans have changed. Please do not call."

There's something delicious and frightening about how easy it seems to drop a person out of your life, whether you know him ten years or ten minutes.

I close my eyes and imagine the sound of a ship's engine pumping, the huge ocean liner sweeping toward tomorrow's destination, but the captain doesn't always take us where we expect.

Life seems awfully complicated.

7

MY EYES POP open. Six-thirty A. M., four and a half hours of sleep, what am I doing up? Hey, it's my first morning in Manhattan, no wonder I'm excited! Funny thing, I didn't dream of the Charlie Chaplin boy.

Ruth's asleep, half smiling, probably off in Dreamsville shopping for furniture with Herman. Nadine's face asleep looks rumpled, not nearly so pretty, and is that a snore I hear? Nadine Jorgensen snores? I feel renewed.

A pile of rumpled blankets on Toni's bed seems like she's hiding under them, but on closer inspection I see she's not there, or in the bathroom either. Also moved is the furniture she pushed against the front door last night.

I wonder what Vic Uris looks like without his face painted white.

Then I throw on my sophisticated black knit dress cinched around by a wide patent leather belt, black suede pumps, black shoulderbag with flashy geometric cutouts, and for a touch of the unexpected, tight gloves in a blazing blue color with bright metal grommets.

The unexpected has a lot to do with style. And style is where the excitement is, according to Ms. Garfield.

Going down in the elevator I notice I'm not thinking

about Matt. Why do I always think I should be thinking about him because we are going steady, and then put myself down because I'm wasting precious moments of life thinking about not thinking about him?

With me in the elevator (which must have been fixed by magic genies in the middle of the night) stands the bellhop who tells me his name is Jerome. He now seems much nicer than yesterday when he was all smirky.

"Noo Yawk is a great town, the greatest," he says, "and I wooden live nowheres else, but you godda have eyes inna backa yaw head, ya hear? Ya godda not trust nobody. Specially ya never been here before. It's a great town, it makes anywheres else like livin' in a cemetery, but it's dog eat dog. You listenin'? You're not listenin'. Nobody listens."

As I spill myself out of the elevator, there's Toni acting chummy with a young guy in a dark gray suit behind the hotel desk. The young guy is older than what we usually mean by a young guy.

"Trisha," she sings out with a voice all champagne bubbles, "this is Peter Parker. Peter, this is my best friend, Trisha Sargent."

Peter Parker, unfortunately, reminds me of the scarecrow in the *Wizard of Oz*. His hair looks like straw sticking out in all directions, and he has a lanky body, black buttons for eyes, and when he turns around I notice he is getting bald in the back.

"Nice meeting you, Peter. Maybe I'll see you to-night," Toni purrs to him and waves.

Then, as we plunk into seats in the hotel coffee shop, she adds, "Isn't he *excellent*?"

"Peter Parker?"

"Of course. Who else? Did you notice his eyes?"

"His eyes? What about his eyes?"

"The way his eyes burn right through you."

"Oh."

"You didn't like his eyes?"

"Toni, I didn't say I didn't like his eyes."

"You didn't have to say it. You think he's too old for me, don't you? Well, he's only twenty-four. He's working as a night clerk while he goes to school in the day. He only has one more year of college. I think seven years is a very good difference in age for a man and woman."

I nod. I don't say what I am thinking. If you want to keep your friends you have to sometimes not say what you are thinking.

Outside the coffee shop window there is a bag lady wearing two dirty knitted caps and three lumpy sweaters, her face ageless, slowly pushing a wire cart piled high with paper bags stuffed with clothing. She is dreamily puffing a corncob pipe. Two tall beautiful young women with high cheekbones and rainbow sweatbands, one in a lavender, the other in a lemon jogging outfit, bounce athletically past the bag lady.

"Isn't it wonderful? Better than a movie!"

"Huh?"

Toni waves her hand admiringly at the street outside the coffee shop window. The bag lady picks up a cigarette butt from the sidewalk and pockets it. The beautiful, tall joggers vanish toward Fifth Avenue, then come three guys gabbing away in white plastic hardhats, and then two nuns in steel-rimmed spectacles and dazzling smiles . . . the people keep streaming past the coffee shop window.

"What'll it be, ladies?" The waitress who takes our orders has an enormous pile of almost orange-colored hair and a wide purple mouth. "I recommend the waffles with sausage links and maple syrup. We got the best waffles—worth getting tooth decay for."

When she brings our order, she puts the plates down as soft as feathers landing on the black formica, and she asks, "You girls with that high school from Cleveland?"

I nod, uncertain how to interpret the sharp glitter in her blue porcelain eyes.

"Seventh floor?"

Again we nod.

"Do me a favor. I'm in the room next to you. The noise last night sounded like World War Five. Got to keep the noise a little human, okay? Sure, your first night I understand you're all excited. Night clerk told me, so I stuffed my head between two pillows. But I have to *sleep*. My husband came up here from where we live in Scranton for a couple of days to look for a job, and he disappeared—poof! So I left my kid with my mama and I'm here to find him, and I'm not giving up till I do. So tonight, please, no more with the noise. Just say to yourselves, 'Hey, Eleanor's next door. She's got to sleep so she can keep looking for her husband Jimmy John.'"

When Eleanor leaves us, Toni giggles. "Don't you just love this city? There's something always happening!"

I don't answer Toni. I'm feeling Eleanor's story. It's awfully sad. How come Toni thinks it's exciting instead of sad? I bet because she has Peter Parker on the brain.

I want to fling myself hungrily into every minute of life, soak up adventure and romance, yet every time I get close to it, with Matt and everyone, a curtain comes down and I hold most of me back behind the curtain.

Would it be different with a stranger like Vic Uris?

Could it be different with Matt?

Anyway, we all meet in the lobby, and Ms. Garfield seems chipper and bouncy—like her thing with Jack Malamud never existed—collecting our first day's production of notebook drawings.

Before we leave the hotel, a telegram and a huge box of dried fruits arrives for Ruth. Herman Katzenellenbogen strikes again. Matt smiles at me from his table with Fat Jack and Teddy. What does he see in those two? Matt yawns as Toni and I leave for the lobby. Nadine, deep in a plush chair in the lobby and leafing through a magazine, also yawns. I put his yawn together with her yawn and I get a paranoid image of Matt and Nadine snuggling together on a sofa and yawning together. Trisha, you're a moron!

Traveling on the Lexington Avenue subway to the Metropolitan Museum of Art is like being in the guts of a dirty monster that screams loud enough to assassinate your eardrums. Our group, minus Miss Carter (who was not feeling so hot), sticks together like glue in the subway. Especially Toni, whose dewy-eyed Peter Parker look has been replaced with the scared darting glances of someone who knows beyond all doubt that she is fated to be mugged at least once and probably three or four times in the jungles of Manhattan.

The museum is a complete other world from the subway. That's what grabs me about New York—so many opposite worlds colliding. Stately fountains, cobblestones and trees and wooden benches, the widest stone steps I've ever walked up, high Greek columns, and rippling bright banners two stories high that name the newest exhibitions.

"You're on your own for the next two hours. Look, explore, walk your feet off, until you find a painting, a sculpture, a piece of jewelry or fabric or pottery that makes you feel alive. The key word is alive. Style is alive, and living is always dangerous. Taste is safe, acceptable, but basically dead. Most of us choose taste, good taste, but we pay the price, because we're less alive."

Matt and I go wandering off together. His fingers knit into mine as we drift through the rooms, corridors, light filtering down from high ceilings and windows. The colors and shapes and textures of things find their way into me, especially the faces in marble of Greek and Roman men and women, centuries old. They don't look happy. They don't look in love. Maybe *in love* is a lot harder to find than I think.

In love. You see it in movies, TV, you read it in books—but where is it when you look for it on the street or in people's houses?

I mean, sure, I think my parents are in love, but they don't talk about it or seem very romantic either. I sort of know it's there, or at least hope it is for them.

In that cavernous museum, sketching, hardly talking, Matt and I occasionally lean against each other, close. Even with all the other museumgoers around, my body vibrates when his body is near, my nerves jump, my heart pumps faster, and at the same time that I yearn to put my mouth against his, I also get angry that anybody should have the power to make me so twitchy and melting.

So, naturally, when my feelings get that way, an argument is always a great way to shake things up.

"That painting is dead as a doornail!"

"Happens to be a great painting, Trisha."

"Why, because it's a Gainsborough?"

"It's great because it's beautiful."

"What does it *do* for you, Matt?"

"Well, up until the moment I saw it hanging on the wall there, I was dying to take my shoe off and scratch my right foot, but one look at that painting and *Wham!* the itch was gone."

"Har-har! I hereby grant you a lifetime membership in the Royal Society of Cretins!"

"Will you admit you like to argue for the sake of arguing?"

"I refuse to say anything until I speak to my lawyer."

"Come on, Trisha. Look at that other Gainsborough painting. Doesn't it take your breath away?"

"It takes away my will to live."

"Why do you have to disagree with the whole world? Gainsborough's paintings sell for hundreds of thousands of dollars."

"You just hate to be challenged, Matt."

"Me? Challenge? I love it. Especially with milk and sugar. Challenge, the breakfast of champions!"

He puts his arm around me. I try to shake him off, but not very hard. Gainsborough's "Blue Boy" stares down at us from a richly carved frame. Matt brushes his mouth across my ear and cheek, then touches his lips to the edge of my mouth. I shiver, fighting back an urge to clamp my arms around his neck and crush my mouth into his.

Gently, I disengage myself from his arm. We walk some more in silence. The faces on the paintings are like an audience waiting for something to happen between Matt and me.

"Matt, do you mind if I look around myself for a while?"

He manages to look delighted. Maybe a little too delighted. We head in different directions.

Is he heading for Nadine?

The moment I'm alone I start cruising for a telephone booth. Before I find one, I happen to see Nadine with Ruth, way down at the far end of a long corridor, sketching a lifesize naked bronze lady. I know Nadine is nothing but a user, but at the moment finding a phone booth leaves me no time to rescue Ruth from whatever evil plan is wriggling around in Nadine's gray matter.

A wide display case of Chinese pottery hundreds of years old stops me for a moment, one peacock blue tea cup as alive as the day it was glazed and fired.

In the main hall below me, Ms. Garfield has arrived early to wait for us. She fingers a beige envelope. She opens the tongue of the envelope and stretches out the beige notepaper.

Why does it bother me that she's still hanging on to that letter from Jack Malamud?

Men may not be the most sensitive creatures on the planet, but they sure can cause a lot of confusion.

My dime drops into the telephone slot and my index

finger starts dialing Vic Uris's home number. What's that old-fashioned voice telling me I'm a jerk to chase him? Well, one look at Vic Uris, you know he's trouble, problems, different. Different, for sure. Maybe different is what I need to jolt me out of a nearly seventeen-year-old rut. Maybe if I don't get jolted now, I'll never get another chance.

The phone rings, clicks, and again I hear his recorded voice: "Welcome to the land of Vic Uris..."

This time, which I know is my last try, my message goes: "Pocahantas, alias the Blue Mouse, will sail from Forty-second Street on the Circle Line at three P.M. Agent X4Z, please make contact onboard, incognito. Secrecy must be preserved at all costs."

8

ENGINES KICKING FOAM behind us, the green and white boat swings away from its Hudson River mooring and downstream into the busy passage of tugs, barges, sailboats, and oil tankers.

"He was born in an army hospital in Frankfurt, Germany." Toni's voice interferes with my scanning the crowd on board for a sign of Vic Uris. "He can't stand being a night clerk, but it's better than driving a cab."

Actually, Toni is talking to Matt who is leaning between her and me on the polished wooden railing of the Circle Line tour boat. The Manhattan skyline slides past; an amplified voice rings over the loudspeakers:

"And if you look to starboard, folks, you see there on the Jersey side of the Hudson River an enormous neon coffee cup with one drop of coffee falling from the lip. That one neon drop is large enough to fill two thousand, seven hundred and fifty-seven normal cups of coffee."

Every time my roving eye hits a target the size and shape and approximate age of Vic Uris, a pang of hope shoots through me. But so far the hope seems hopeless. One character I thought might be Vic turned out to be a very angry girl when she turned around; another proved to be a young red-faced priest.

"Care for a coconut bar, Trisha?"

Ruth, to my left, smiles so contentedly that I relax my eye-hopping search for Vic Uris.

"There's nothing more depressing than the wrong kind of coconut bar," she says profoundly. A warm light pools in her face. "Herman always gets me the right kind."

"Ruth, you're wonderful."

Her eyes widen as if I just said that she had a spider on her left eyebrow.

"You're always so mellow," I explain.

"Not when my hair bothers me. My nerves get terrible."

I'm about to explain that even her hair anxiety seems relaxed in comparison to the rest of us females, but there's someone walking toward the bow of the boat, shoulders exactly as I remember Vic Uris, a huge floppy wide-brimmed leather hat obscuring his face and hair.

I squeeze Matt's arm and murmur, "Be right back."

I stroll aft, past the snack counter amidship, and reach the bow, where the leather hat is under a lifeboat slung overhead near the starboard railing. A green feather flutters in the band of the hat as the breeze from Brooklyn flows across the bow.

I circle around to the port bow railing for a front view of him. I don't want to be disappointed. Suppose it is Vic Uris and he doesn't think I'm as attractive today as I was yesterday? Or suppose his face without makeup and an audience leaves me blah?

The person in the leather hat cranes his neck as if he too expects to meet someone on board. He has a thick black beard and a knobby misshapen nose and dark glasses. I give up, turn away. Dozens of white seagulls hang effortlessly in the airstream overhead. Okay, drop this Vic Uris business, will you, Trisha? Concentrate on the low, lonely silhouettes of oil tankers anchored out toward Staten Island. And the greenish lady to starboard draped in long folds of bronze, her torch of liberty thrust toward the clouds. Sad lady if ever I saw one.

"I am vanting to telling you a shtory, hokay?"

A thick guttural Russian voice sounds close behind me. The voice comes from the huge black beard, the leather hat, the dark glasses.

My feet are poised to run a four-minute mile. "Are you speaking to me?"

"Eef you are eggscusing me, I yam spikking to you!"

"Look, I'm sorry, but I—"

The frame of his dark glasses, pinched between two fingers, slides down to the tip of his enormous pasty nose. Those deepset gray-blue eyes—*his* eyes!

"Are you who I think you are?"

"You haff said ve must mitt in secret, no?"

When I'd seen him up close yesterday there was a piercing yet tender quality to his eyes, a danger. Now his eyes seem softer, the color of the sea on a cloudy morning.

For a moment we say nothing. The throb of the engines and the sway of the river as the boat maps a wide arc past a small island seem to join us together as if we are partners in a motionless dance.

"You vant hearing my shtory, comrade? Vas vunts a men sikking visdom...he gots himself running from hungry tiger, at edge of tousand foots cliff he trips and falls ofer cliff but grabs hold root of shtrawberry plant. So on one side of the men iss tiger, udder side is tousand-foots drop to rocks. Along comes two little brown mices, they shtart chewing dee root in halfs. Just that moment the men sees beautiful ripe shtrawberry growing. He reach up with teeth and bite into shtrawberry. Never he tasted such miracle shtrawberry in whole life!"

I love listening to his Russian accent.

"You like shtory?"

"How does it end?"

He drops his Russian accent, and his voice returns to the way I remember it, kind of smoky. "The story ends when the strawberry tastes wonderful."

"I don't get it."

He leans closer. Now I see, tucked in under his black wig under the floppy leather hat, a curl of wavy gold hair.

"That's okay. I enjoyed telling it. Did you enjoy listening?"

"You're weird."

"Good weird or bad weird?"

"Medium weird."

"I'm having a party tonight. Will you come?"

"I can't tonight. Also, I should tell you I'm going steady with a boy from my school who is on this boat. We're a senior art and fashion class from Cleveland, and—"

"If you won't come to my party, will you at least say yes when I ask you to marry me?"

"Tomorrow morning at seven-thirty we're planning to leave our hotel and go jogging up Fifth Avenue and into Central Park."

"We?"

"My teacher and some of the girls I came with."

"Do I have to meet you incognito again?"

I nod my head. "Why are we starting something that can't possibly go anywhere?"

Vic murmurs, "Because we're crazy, but a nice crazy."

"Your beard is slipping."

He adjusted his beard. "Just remember, when the two little brown mice start chewing the root, you taste the most delicious strawberry in the world."

For an instant, as the Circle Line sightseeing boat veers around the southern tip of Manhattan Island and the crackly loudspeaker voice points out Wall Street and the Fulton Fish Market and the Brooklyn Bridge strung with cables that look like a gigantic harp waiting to be plucked by some god or goddess, for just those few moments Vic Uris, in spite of his fake beard and lopsided putty nose, seems to be a small boy standing far away down the end of a long dark corridor, a candle in one hand and a rigid little curlicue smile on his lips, peering into the darkness as if he expected to see someone who had promised to solve every problem a little boy could possibly have.

But maybe that's not him at all, that little boy— maybe that's only what I'd like him to be.

"And during the early years of Dutch rule, before the British occupation of the city, those piers you see on our port side, ladies and gentlemen, were the site of—"

A glimpse of Ms. Garfield and a knot of seniors climbing down the metal stairs from the upper deck sends a jolt of fear through me.

"If my teacher thinks I'm meeting someone, we'll *never*—" I whisper urgently.

Vic winks, flicks his dark glasses back into place, strolls away across the deck, and disappears up the stairs to starboard.

The boat continues upstream along the East River, past so many interesting, colorful, memorable places, but I don't see any of them, even though my eyes are open.

I lean into the rail, wondering what it is about Vic Uris that makes me so desperately willing to make a fool of myself.

9

RUSH HOUR, THE Sixth Avenue subway. One great thing about New York is that even when you have to line up in a long snake of people to buy a subway token there's always somebody interesting to see. But I find myself even more interested in wondering if Vic is a senior or just graduating or maybe a dropout.

Then through the turnstile, the entire Cleveland contingent except Miss Carter (whose niece seems delighted by the news that the doctor ordered her aunt to bed for the day).

Another flight of dingy stairs takes us, along with the river of other bodies, deeper into the bowels of Manhattan. Ms. Garfield's advice just before we got our baptism of fire in the rush hour was: "Keep your arms in front of you, both hands on your handbag, and don't scream or kick anybody unless you're absolutely sure he is pinching you on purpose."

To which Matt asks, "What if the *he* is a *she*?" Of course, Teddy and Fat Jack crack up.

How old is Vic? He could be a young twenty or a very mature seventeen.

The train screeches down the track toward us. Shoulders to the right of you, shoulders to the left of you, spines to the front of you. The door slides open and several passengers claw their way through the human barrier. Wait, there's no room in this car! The words are forming on my lips when an irrepressible tide of bodies bashes us forward into the crushed bodies already inside the car, bodies which miraculously manage, squeezing and muttering, to accept thirty or forty more sardines. The doors skid shut.

Comrade, I am vanting to tell you a shtory. He isn't sexy, that's what's odd. It isn't his eyes or voice or hair or nose or muscles that give me such a peculiar feeling when I'm with him. It's more like he is a very special music, like the Pied Piper, and I just want to go where he goes.

Sometimes, when the train slows at a station, the scream of the brakes is so loud that you feel your eardrums are about to split.

Toni, Matt, and I are squeezed so tightly together we're practically breathing each other's breath.

"Isn't New York thrilling?" I tease Toni in a whisper.

"Peter says he wouldn't live anywhere else in the world," she replies proudly, but then her face contorts and her eyes pop open and she hisses close to my ear in a mixture of panic and fury: "Somebody is rubbing my leg!"

I check out the possible rapists immediately behind Toni. One rapist is an old lady with an umbrella, and the other is a fat lady wheezing with the weight of a rolled-up furry rug.

"Be cool, Toni," I advise softly. "It's only a rug."

Matt grins, and the feel of his body pressed so close to mine in the crush of the crowd makes me look away from him. Is there a psychologist in the audience? I wonder whether lasting relationships are better when they begin from the beginning with one person causing lots of romantic feelings in the other person, like with Matt, or when it is sort of mysterious and hypnotic between people like with Vic?

"Mmmm." Matt smiles as the rocketing train sags us

back and forth against each other. "I can see why people like Manhattan." He winks slyly at me.

The stacked heel of my shoe happens to come down hard on the soft beige toe of his desert boot.

"OW! Hey! Who—"

"My heel has a crush on your toe," I whisper sweetly to him.

Matt leans closer, so close that his mouth touches my eyelashes. I can't resist or get away; my arms are clasped at my side. I really don't want to, either. The lights black out in the car suddenly. I close my eyes and surrender to the motion of the train as it thunders along the track, and to the closeness of Matt. I feel his lips on my ear. I want him to stop but I also want him to go on. The rocking train swings us apart and together again. I twist my head, so his mouth is back on my eyelashes. The lights blink on. Toni sniffs at us, annoyed. "That's what I mean about older men—they have enough sense not to nibble your eyelashes in public!"

"A man gets chased by a tiger," I say to both of them, "and falls off a cliff and grabs hold of a root, so he's hanging from the root a thousand feet over sharp rocks, and the tiger's jaws are only inches away. Just at that moment two brown mice begin chewing through the root, and the man sees a little red strawberry growing near it and he snatches the strawberry between his teeth. The strawberry tastes marvelous."

"So?"

"That's the end of the story."

Matt pulls a wry face. "Dumb story."

"I think it's very significant," I snap at him. "Toni, what do you think?"

The train crashes along the tracks into the West Fourth Street station. Toni says something I can't hear. Doors bang open, bodies go spinning out onto the platform. "Everybody here?" Ms. G. counts heads.

Upstairs and outside on Sixth Avenue, Ms. Garfield,

with great relish, leads us along Waverly Place to the huge stone monument in Washington Square Park, an arch flanked by two statues of George W. "You're on your own for dinner. This is the heart of Greenwich Village. We'll meet back here in two hours. Okay, synchronize watches!"

"Come with me!" Matt commands, his strong hand taking mine prisoner, and before I can get my plans together with Toni and Ruth, he sweeps me away between the two Georges, under the stone arch and across the cobblestones, past a circular fountain and on through the park to MacDougal Street. Actually, I sort of like being swept away, so I don't object really. Matter of fact, maybe Matt should do even more sweeping than he does.

"You're a good sweeper, Matt."

I don't think he hears me. I love his face when it gets that determined look, jaw jutting forward that way. I love the broad slope of his shoulders. I love a lot of things about Matt, so how come I don't think I'm in love?

For one thing, dummy, if you're in love with someone you don't arrange secret meetings with the Pied Piper.

By now our Cleveland crew is out of sight. A steady stream of sneaker people is pounding the pavement that surrounds the park. A yellow frisbee whips through the air over the heads of the chess players on this corner of the park. A boy with a lion's mane of hair plays his guitar like he's shooting a machine gun, and sings raspy-voiced to a casual audience. A flutist in African dress makes jazz music, accompanied by a bongo drummer. There's a long-haired young girl kissing a short-haired boy on a bench. There's a shaved-head young girl kissing a long-haired young man on the grass.

Matt stops me. "Dirt on your cheek."

"Where?"

Matt rubs my cheek. His arms slide around me. His

mouth covers mine. I want to push him away. Kissing at a crowded corner of a crowded park of a crowded city without even asking me is...is— I sink into the kiss, my heart banging away like a car doing fifty with a flat tire.

When he takes his mouth away, I have trouble getting words out, it's hard to catch my breath. He *knows* I've been shook up by his kiss, and he *winks* at me, which makes me really mad.

"I wish you'd ask me, Matt."

"Ask you what?"

"Before you kiss me."

"Didn't you like it?"

"Yes."

"So? We *are* going steady."

"There's more to a relationship than just kissing."

"I hope so," he grins wryly, suggestively.

"That's not funny, Matt!"

"I meant friendship, cooperation, understanding, helping each other with homework, that kind of thing."

"That's not what you meant, Matt."

"I did, I swear!" He makes a three-fingered Boy Scout salute, his face tightening into a phony soldierly expression. "A scout is trustworthy, loyal, helpful, friendly, courteous, kind, obedient, cheerful, thrifty, brave, clea—"

"You can eat by yourself, Matt Hartman!"

"Come on, Trisha, I was only kidding!"

"I want to be alone and think."

"Hey." He reaches for my wrist. "Thinking is more fun when you do it *with* someone."

"Matt, I mean it. I need to be alone. I'm confused."

"What about?"

"If I knew, I wouldn't need to think about it."

"I'll help you think, Trisha." That comfortable strong arm of his slipping protectively around my shoulder has a surprising power of persuasion, but I slip out from under it.

"Thinking is something you have to do alone, Matt."

"That's not always true."

"Of course it is!"

"Look at all those scientists who pool their research and have those think-tanks."

"We're arguing again. Why are we arguing?"

"Because arguing is fun."

"I hate arguing!"

"Trisha, I've known you a long time. You *love* arguing."

"*Now* we're arguing about arguing!"

"Hey, don't be so serious!"

"I *want* to be serious!"

"Okay, be serious! Man! What's got into you, Trisha?"

I've never seen Matt's face so guarded, his forehead wrinkled, eyes hooded, almost slits, lips pushed forward as if he was about to spit.

"I didn't mean to make you so angry, Matt."

"Who's angry? I'm not angry, I'm perfectly calm." His eyes blaze at me.

"You look angry."

"That's your opinion, Trisha! You've always got to be right, don't you?"

My voice peeks out small and soft and apologetic. "I'm sorry, Matt."

Ooh, do I despise myself when my voice comes out apologetic while my insides are dropping nuclear bombs!

But it does work with Matt. And my father too, come to think of it.

His shoulders, all bunched tight and high, relax, and the fierceness in his face washes away. "I'm sorry, too. Look, Trish, I'll meet you later, okay?"

He taps one finger to his forehead and peels off down MacDougal Street.

Casually, I glance up at the sky-tangled branches of high old trees, their tiny April leaves making a new green beginning. What's beginning for you Trisha?

10

WANDERING AROUND Greenwich Village over to Christopher Street and Sheridan Square all by myself, peering at menus on the windows of dozens of intimate little restaurants, my salivary glands beginning to operate full-blast, isn't as great as I hoped it would be.

I thought I'd be thinking interesting romantic thoughts about New York and me and Vic Uris and Matt, but instead of those thoughts I am thinking about how lonely it is to be alone, and where's all the romance when you're one instead of two?

The thing about Matt is I've known him so long there isn't anything I don't know about him. But with Vic I want to know so much.

I pass enticing little stores tucked into each little street, dozens of them—a store stocked with barrels and barrels of old-fashioned candies, a bakery displaying Earth Mother bread and Cosmic Consciousness cookies, a furniture store where the lamps and couches and tables look straight out of Star Wars—and the couples I see leaning toward each other across the tables in the glassed-in restaurants make me jealous.

Vic, were you born in Manhattan? What do your parents do? Have you brothers or sisters? How do you feel about women's liberation? Nuclear war? *Hill Street Blues*? Cheese omelettes?

A broken teacup painted on a plain white wooden board hangs over the entrance to—of course—a little restaurant called the Broken Teacup, blocks west of where Matt and I parted. It's the only place so far I've peered into that looks like it won't annihilate my budget. And the inside smells deliciously of spices and homemade soup and hamburger.

But only one empty table. *And* it's not empty; a coat lies thrown over a chair. A familiar coat. A girl's coat, the shade of green exactly right for platinum blond hair. It's too late to run, because Nadine waltzes out of the ladies room as if she just won a gold medal for Viking Queen of the Year.

"Hi, Trisha!"

"I was just leaving."

"Why? It isn't any fun eating alone." She doesn't sound as sophisticated as she usually tries to sound, and her face, instead of its usual sleek winner's look, seems almost ordinary.

"I'd like to know why you don't like me, Trisha."

A round little waitress flutters around us nervously, mouth trying out different sizes and shapes of welcoming smiles.

"I'll have a marshmallow fudge ice cream sundae, one scoop of vanilla, one chocolate," Nadine says firmly.

"I don't think we have that," the waitress mumbles, shooting her apologetic eyes at the menu just in case she is wrong.

"Well, I'm sure you can make it even if it's not on the menu," Nadine insists frostily.

"Nadine, this is your *supper*. Couldn't you have something normal?" I urge, glancing toward the waitress, who gives the impression that hot coals are being applied to her bare feet.

"This is my first waitress job." The woman worriedly

smooths out her striped uniform. "I told them I had a year's experience."

"All right," Nadine relents. "I'll have buckwheat cakes with maple syrup and extra butter and two three-minute softboiled eggs on the side."

A rubbery smile stretches the waitress's lips as she scribbles speedily on her check pad. The point of her pencil shatters; she looks like she's on a sinking ship as she bites frantically at the tip of the pencil.

"I'll have a cheeseburger, please, with a tossed salad."

She writes with the chewed pencil, then scoots away.

"I hope she keeps the job."

"She's trying to put something over on the boss. She should have told him the truth."

"That's exactly one of the reasons I don't like you, Nadine. You don't seem to care about other people's problems."

"I care."

"You never show it."

What shocks the socks off me is that she doesn't get hostile when I tell her what I think, and she actually seems to be seriously listening.

"I guess I don't show it."

"Believe me, Nadine"—I hammer the nail home with all the irritation I've ever felt toward her—"you don't seem to care about anyone but you!"

It's obvious that what I say hurts her, because the light dims in those blue eyes of hers and there is the tiniest tremor in her lips.

"Maybe I need a friend like you to teach me."

"Get off it, Nadine! What kind of an act are you pulling?"

"It's not an act, Trisha."

"You throw yourself at Matt every chance you get, ever since he and I started going steady, and you've got the nerve to say you need me as a friend?"

"I can't help it if I'm attracted to Matt. I guess I never

realized how much I liked him until he fell for you. And I'm not going to stop trying to take him away from you. But we could still be friends."

"I don't believe I'm hearing this! You're warped, you know that? You must think I'm a moron or something."

"I just want to be honest with you. I was talking with Ruth and she told me what a good friend you are to her, and I was jealous because I never had a friend."

Sudden tears spill from her eyes. She shoves away from the table, and vanishes into the ladies room.

That's what I call a complicated person. I mean, really, isn't there *anybody* who doesn't have problems?

And oddly, of all the people I know right now, she'd probably be the easiest one to tell about my kooky feelings for Vic Uris.

Vic's face sits in my mind, and then I see Matt and Ms. Garfield, Toni and her night clerk, the bald bus-driver, Ruth and Herman, the waitress looking for her husband, Jerome the bellhop, the bag lady, poor skinny unmarried Miss Carter. Why does everybody have to have problems?

Nadine returns, very pale, worried. "Could you help me find my contact lens? I dropped it in the ladies room."

I follow her. Contact lens, huh? Next thing it'll be that her Viking hair is a wig. It is weird to find out that the gorgeous Nadine Jorgensen wears contact lenses and snores and worries about not having friends. Luckily, inside the ladies room, I find her lens right away.

When we're back at the table, I dig into my cheese-burger, which has been sitting on the table, but Nadine waves the waitress over and brusquely says, "Please have my plate heated up!"

The fluttery waitress squeaks, "I don't think the cook is going to like that." Nadine glares at her, and the wait-ress's jittery hands reach for Nadine's plate, hoist it up at just the wrong angle, and one slightly cold pile of hotcakes with two soft-boiled eggs on the side slip off the plate to find their resting place in the pearl gray lap of Nadine's skirt.

Why at that moment—as Nadine sits there frozen and the scared waitress smiles woodenly—does it occur to me that Vic Uris must hand out his card to thousands of impressionable girls on the street just the way he did to me?

Well, whatever happens with Vic Uris, I'll always have at least one beautiful memory of New York: Nadine Jorgensen with soft-boiled eggs in her lap.

11

FEET, HUGE PAIRS of distorted feet, some yellow, some green, painted in vivid angles on a wall-size canvas facing me. One pair of feet has two toes pincering a burning filter-tip cigarette, and the cigarette is burning the sole of the foot above it.

It's a retrospective showing of Jack Malamud's paintings, and we still can't believe Ms. Garfield managed to get all of us personally invited by the artist himself.

Gliding in front of me, a white-haired woman in a gold lamé dress stares at the cigarette-smoking foot and remarks to a stunningly handsome tuxedoed man half her age, "So I simply told her she shouldn't feel guilty about having a facelift."

Cigarette smoke hangs in clouds. It's as crowded as the subway was in the rush hour, except that here people seem to enjoy rubbing elbows. Nadine would probably love it, but she and her soft-boiled skirt are back at our hotel by now.

Jack Malamud's paintings are pretty violent, bloody, twisted shapes, colors that fling themselves at you. So you kind of expect the man who painted them to be a tall, swaggering, wild-eyed artist type, but he turns out instead to be sort of pink and pudgy and sweet, balding, clouds of wispy gray hair on the sides of his head, glasses down at the tip of a cute nose, kind of a cross between a mischievous elf and a kindly old family doctor.

He hasn't let go of Ms. Garfield's arm since he practically fell over himself to get to her when we arrived. Ms. Garfield wears a mysterious half-smile as he guides her in and out of the crowd, lots of people shaking his hand admiringly, but he has eyes for no one but Ms. G.

I wonder if Matt would carry a torch for me if we ever split?

The hubbub of sophisticated talk, the restless mixture of sneakers and high heels, evening gowns and sweatbands, tuxedos and cheap denims—it all reminds me that there's a lot more in the world than you see from our little suburb in Cleveland, almost like I've been inside a cocoon my whole life, playing good-girl-nice-girl, more or less, not really taking any risks.

Vic Uris is definitely a risk.

I catch a glimpse of Ruth looking intense and lonely as she meanders into another room of the gallery, where Jack Malamud's sculptures are on display. Matt is nowhere around. He and I haven't talked since our argument; I was planning to apologize to Matt and ask him if he found a nice place to eat, but when our group met after dinner and began walking south from the arch, Matt hung back, avoiding me, joking loudly with Teddy and Fat Jack, and then as we flooded into the gallery entrance he disappeared, which Ms. Garfield was too preoccupied to notice.

"Trisha, I'm going back to the hotel." Toni grabs my arm. "Ms. Garfield says it's okay."

"You're crazy! This is what we came to New York for. This is the art world. If you were watching it on TV, you'd be glued to the tube!"

"If I leave now," she explained slyly, "I'll get back to the hotel just about when Peter comes on duty."

"Mind if I give you a piece of advice?"

"You're going to tell me he's too old."

"Toni, this is New York. People are much more so-phisticated here."

"I can take care of myself!" Toni whirls her back toward me, squeezing away through the art watchers. Teddy Jackson tries to talk to her but she shrugs him off, and he stands there listlessly combing his pompadour.

I feel like such a jerk. Who am I to ram advice down Toni's throat? What about me and Vic Uris? Aren't I acting just as dumb as Toni? Except that I don't get panicky the way she does when things go blooey.

I follow her out onto the street, but not to stop her. I snake my way through the pedestrians—this is SoHo, clustered with glittery boutiques, chic restaurants, half-a-dozen art galleries per inch. I walk over to a phone, pay, dial a number, ring, ring, ring, and then a voice I know says, "Hello, so what's with you?"

"This is Cleveland."

"How are things in Ohio?"

"I'm not sure. How are things in Manhattan?"

"Close your eyes, Trisha."

"Why?"

"I didn't hear your eyes close."

"They're closed."

"Okay, now think like you are lost in the Sahara Desert, you ain't seen nothing alive for a week. You're starving, your waterbag is empty. Suddenly there's a monster roadsign stuck in a sand dune. The sign says, 'Eat at Vic's. Friendly Food. Hamburgers That Never Let Your Cheese Get Lonely.'"

I'm smiling all over the phone. "You're funny."

"I better be."

"But I don't know anything about you."

"What would you like to know?"

"Are you still in high school? How old are you? Why do you entertain on the street? What else do you do? What music do you like? Does it bother you that I have a steady boyfriend? Were you born in Manhattan? Do you have brothers or sisters?"

"Is that all the questions?"

"For a while."

"Hey, I'll tell you everything you want to know tomorrow, how's that?"

"Are you saying you have to hang up now?"

"I most definitely ain't."

"Good, because I have to hang up now."

We both laughed. "Who hangs up first?" I asked.

"I count to three, we both hang up the same time. Ready? One . . . two . . . three!"

Neither of us hang up. I hear his breathing. He whispers into the phone, "The mice are really spaced out chewing that vine, and the strawberry tastes wild."

Slowly, gently, I cradle my receiver. If Ms. Garfield finds me missing, I might never find out what the strawberry really means.

12

BACK AT THE Hotel Manhattan, I find Toni flipping through a magazine and darting impatient glances at Peter Parker, who seems very aloof and businesslike in his charcoal suit as he registers three burly men who have thick accents you can cut with a knife and look to me like Nazi storm troopers in disguise.

Peter, darting a glance over at Toni, hands me a phone message from my parents and a note left by a Mr. Zarkan Eleftherides, Jr.

The message from Mom and Pop says: "Hope you had a great trip. If there's anything you need, give us a call."

Why should that make me feel so resentful? Because they try to be so *nice*, I guess, instead of saying straight out what is really on their minds. Like: "You forgot to call when you arrived, and we don't like it!"

On the other hand, they *are* at least trying to be kind— but I do think I'm old enough so that I don't have to call home the minute I arrive somewhere! Hold your horses, Trisha, a voice says, you've been at the hotel two days already; your folks deserve a call.

Two days? I feel like I've known Vic a lifetime. New York has a way of crowding things together so fast.

And these *voices* inside you, always there to remind you of what you *should* have done or what you *should* do. I'd like to kick those voices out forever.

Hey, what's got into you, Trisha? The voices only want you to understand that your parents have feelings too.

So I decide to send them a telegram. Why don't I feel like talking to them? I love them both, of course, but for the first time in my life I feel almost completely on my own, anything can happen, and I don't want to be reminded that I'm only almost seventeen. *Only!* In some societies you could have three babies by seventeen.

Also, I guess my sending the telegram instead of phoning them is sort of like saying hey I'm me and I do things my own way now.

Anyway, I'm alone in our room on the seventh floor of the hotel, holding the message left for me by Zarkan Eleftherides, Jr., and wondering what Ruth and Nadine are up to, this late. A few minutes ago Matt knocked on the door, and the two of us apologized to each other, and I told him that I was so exhausted I was going to sleep.

I hear the door next door bang shut. It must be Eleanor the waitress with the teased orange hair. I hope she has found some clues to her missing husband.

The bed is heaven, I'm suddenly so tired, but I read the note from Mr. Zarkan Eleftherides, Jr. twice more before sleep zaps me. It says:

"Hello? Happy who? Don't never say goodbye! You got questions, I got answers. Open sesame! Wanna fall off the cliff with me?"

Zarkan Eleftherides, Jr. is a totally different world from Matt Hartman. I try to skate away from the guilty feelings about walking out on Matt for supper.

I whisper into my pillow, "Zarkan...Vic."

13

FIFTH AVENUE, SEVEN A.M.. Who are those beautiful loonies jogging uptown toward Central Park?

The beautiful loonies pounding the tar with their fashionable neon sneakers are eight female seniors from Cleveland, plus Ms. Garfield.

"I'm dying! My body feels like somebody just dug it up!"

"Watch out for those cars or they'll be planting all of us!" Ms. Garfield calls back over her shoulder from the front position.

Fifth Avenue is one-way downtown, but we are jogging against traffic, following two men joggers who seem to know what they are doing, a straggly line of us on the east side of the tar, gasping uptown past store windows artfully arranged to make you want to buy millions of classy garments and accessories and anything else you can think of.

"How many more blocks to Central Park?"

"Twenty-five."

"We must be out of our minds."

"If my feet have a heart attack, bury me in Saks Fifth Avenue!"

"How come none of the boys are jogging?"

"They're too smart."

"Whose idea was this anyway?"

"Toni's."

"She's not even here!"

"She stayed to talk to that night clerk."

"Hey, Ms. Garfield, that was terrific in the gallery last night."

"Are the people in SoHo always so weird?"

"They probably think we're weird."

Ms. Garfield, out in front of the line and disgustingly enthusiastic, yells back, "Anybody see Nadine?"

Nadine said she'd catch up with us, that she'd broken her shoelace, but I'm thinking it was just an excuse to stay behind and monopolize Matt. I shouldn't be so suspicious. Oh, yes you *should*, Trisha darling, she *told* you she's trying to take Matt away. Who knows, maybe it would be a good thing if she did. Not on your life! Half an hour ago I found a note for me slipped under the door, a note from Matt that said, "My heart is in the right place, even if my brain isn't sometimes."

You don't want to lose a guy like that, Trisha.

But admit it, two guys like Matt and Vic leaving you notes kind of makes you think you are special, doesn't it?

"One thing about Manhattan," Gloria Carter yips sarcastically from behind me, "you really see the beauties of nature."

"Oh, that's so true, the sunlight on a broken beer bottle!"

"The morning dew on a squashed cigarette butt!"

"Hey, I just got my second wind!"

"I haven't even gotten my first yet!"

"Is that all that interests you, breathing? Look at those gorgeous shoes!"

"Big deal! We've got some terrific stores in Cleveland too!"

"I'll bet you the same dress has twice as much style

when you wear it on Fifth Avenue than when you wear it in Cleveland."

"That's really *thick*. Where'd you read that?"

I'm enjoying exerting my body as it gets into stride, but I see Ruth hasn't smiled once since we left the hotel. She has dark patches under her eyes and in place of her usual easygoing cheerfulness her face has a worried sort of gloom.

"Ruth, you all right?"

She keeps doggedly pounding the pavement. "I couldn't get to sleep last night. I started writing Herman a letter four times and each one I tore up. Trisha, I don't know why, but suddenly I began to wonder if I really know the *real* Herman Katzenellenbogen."

I tell you, hearing that shakes me up. Ruth and Herman are my Rock of Gibraltar. If *she's* not sure, there's no hope for any of us.

"WOW! That black gown in Saks!"

"St. Patrick's Cathedral!"

"Who's that statue with the world on his back?"

"That's Arnold Schwarzenegger, stupid!"

"Oooh! Tiffany's!"

"Bergdorf Goodman!"

"There's Nadine!"

And sure enough there's the blonde Viking herself, knees pumping as she obviously aims to pass each and every one of us. Her eyes meet mine for a fraction of a second. It could be my imagination, but for just that one moment beautiful Nadine became that simple normal girl from last night with a simple natural smile who said she'd never had a friend—but only for a split-second.

"What's the difference between a boyfriend and peanut butter?" Nadine shouts brassily as she races ahead.

"Tell us, please, Nadine, pretty please with sugar on it!" several girls retort in a singsong sarcastic chorus.

"A boyfriend doesn't stick to the roof of your mouth!"

"Boooooo!" the girls hoot. "Take her back!"

Nose in the air, Nadine sweeps ahead of Ms. Garfield as the Plaza Hotel looms over us.

Opposite the Plaza there are fancy hansom cabs attached to tired-looking horses, the drivers sporting black top hats, and there is a bizarre guy on roller skates dressed like a pirate with a handlebar mustache, Van Dyke chin whiskers, coal black hair down to his shoulders, and saucer-size dark glasses.

The pirate skater does figure eights as we jog into the park entrance, me last, and one of his figure eights cuts directly alongside me.

"I'm ready to answer all your questions, Pocahantas."

"Vic!" His black wig really fooled me.

I slow down, dropping back farther and farther from the girls ahead, who are curving down the path toward the lake.

"Why don't you want your friends to know about me?"

"If they think I'm slipping away to meet a strange boy, they start gossiping, the teacher starts worrying, and pretty soon I'll be on a plane home."

His eyes crinkle with a wry grin. "So you think I'm strange?"

"You're different."

"I'm just your basic New York weirdo. We come in all sizes, shapes, and colors."

"You're not a weirdo."

"Man, if I'm not a weirdo, what am I?"

"Somebody I really want to know."

"What would you like me to be, Trisha?"

"I think you are probably very honest with your emotions, and I think you want life to be very very special, and you take risks, and you are gentle and . . . and mysterious . . . and—"

I'm puffing and running and talking and amazed at what's coming out of my mouth and at the same time watching the jogging girls ahead of us in case they should look back and see me with Vic, so I'm completely unprepared for Vic's reaction. He skates in front of me, lifts me off my feet and zooms away from the main path, over to an outcropping of rock.

"Wait! Vic! Where are you—"

The asphalt curves downhill and we're picking up speed, me perched in Vic's arms, the clouds and the sky and the tiny new April leaves on the branches overhead spinning past us. And smooth to a stop.

"Please put me down, Vic."

Easily he lowers me until my feet touch the grass. I'm surprised at how strong he is.

"What you said about me, Trisha, did you mean it?"

"I think so."

His face seems so vulnerable I want to reach out and stroke his cheek, but I don't.

"Thanks, Trisha."

"I should be thanking *you*."

"Why?"

I suddenly get so embarrassed I have to turn away so he can't see my face. "I've got to catch up with my class, Vic."

"Agent X4Z to Blue Mouse. Where do we rendezvous tonight?"

I can't put a name to whatever it is that suddenly scares me, but I say, "I don't know if we should meet again, Vic."

Our eyes reach silently toward each other as if we are standing at opposite ends of a long dark tunnel.

"Sure, I understand, Trisha."

"No, you don't."

"Okay, I guess I don't understand."

"Don't be so understanding!"

He can't help grinning, though a shadow falls in the liquid gray-blue of his eyes. "I'll try not to be so understanding."

"Why do I get the idea that I'm a jerk?"

The tip of his tongue rubs back and forth across his

chipped front tooth for a moment, and his voice comes urgent, intense: "Trisha?"

"Yes?"

"Let's be very happy!"

"How, Vic?"

"We'll find a way."

"I'm afraid, Vic."

"So am I."

"I don't know what I feel. About you. About Matt. And when I go back to Cleveland in just a few days, what happens then?"

His eyebrows and shoulders rise, his brow creases, he becomes a hunchbacked little old man scratching his chin in bewilderment, his voice ancient, scratchy. "We'll have to find a tree trunk with a secret door and climb down into the darkness."

He skates away backward, still pantomiming the hunchbacked old man, until his skate catches in a hole and crashes him ignominiously, a tangled heap of legs and skates and arms.

We're both roaring when I get to him, and he murmurs between laughs, "Ain't that the gracefullest you ever seen?"

He lets me help him to his feet. Why is it every time our eyes meet I get the sensation of being a little girl?

"Will you leave a message for me on my machine, where to meet you? I've got to see you tonight."

"I'm not sure I can. Why tonight?"

He quickly straightens up, shoots a salute at me, pantomimes a rifle on his shoulder and snaps: "My outfit might be sent overseas tomorrow to parachute into Nazi-occupied France. This might be the last time we see each other until the war is over."

He swerves away, skates flying.

I race back to the path where we had split off from the other girls. Far ahead I see their colorful jogging suits flash between the trees and rocks of Central Park.

14

"I KNOW IT'S kind of maybe reverse prejudice, but why do I feel that Chinese people are absolutely *never* going to mug me?"

The voice is Toni's. We are in Chinatown, naturally. The bunch of us are threading our way along Canal Street, sidewalks thronged with Oriental faces, boxes of exotic vegetables and fruits and wriggling blue crabs on ice and squid and octopus in front of the stores, the windows splashed with incomprehensible Chinese letters and, in English, names like Hoo Sung Hoo and Wo Fat Kim and Ming Wing Low.

Matt and I are holding hands. I'm more confused than ever because it's breathtaking to go from Vic to Matt to Vic to Matt. Vic seems to accept Matt in my life, but Matt would flip if he knew about Vic. But I love the feel of Matt's hand, so secure, in a crowd like this, like I'm attached to an anchor or something.

I laugh for no real reason. Matt laughs at my laugh. I laugh at his laugh. A couple of nice Chinese people laugh at us laughing.

The last streaks of light are disappearing behind us in the sky, the street is filled with delicious smells of Chinese food, and ahead of us in the east a couple of sedate white stars are doing their thing. Plus there is an actual orange moon shining where we turn right at the corner of Canal and Bowery.

It's funny, in the middle of the crowd, how my head is full of people. I worry about them—all day that's been happening, from the time we got back from jogging and then hit the Museum of Modern Art, making sketches like mad of people and places, I keep thinking of so many different people.

Like Eleanor Roosevelt—that's her real name!—the orange-haired waitress in the room next door who's searching for her husband. Her face seemed so drained when I saw her this morning, but she said, grimly cheerful: "I'll find him!"

And Ruth. I'm very bothered about Ruth because she's got some crazy idea in her head about herself and Herman and I've never seen her looking so deep down inside.

Toni too. I mean, really, she's headed for trouble hanging around that Peter Parker. "He's in *therapy*," Toni dropped on me this afternoon at MOMA, as if being in therapy is the most glamorous thing in the world. "For the last five years, twice a week, and he says it explained everything to him about why his marriage busted up after six months."

Chubby Marcia Carter just keeps smiling all over the place, especially aiming her smile at Fat Jack and his dumb haircut. Can't she see it's hopeless with Jack? And it bothers me that it doesn't seem to bother Marcia that her aunt is still sick back at the hotel.

Nadine keeps throwing me those quick little friendly hopeful looks ever since we talked at the Broken Teacup.

And Jerome the bellhop—he wrinkled his broken nose when I got back from jogging this morning and told me how he's only being a bellhop to save the money to gamble with to hit it big and buy his life's dream, a shoe store.

Believe it or not, I'm even beginning to feel sorry for

Teddy Jackson, in spite of his oily pompadour, because Toni really gives him the ice-cold shoulder now that she's found Peter Parker.

And I worry about the bag lady who passes every morning. I even think sad thoughts about the assistant hotel manager, Mr. Kratz, with his silly dumb toupee.

Above all, there's Ms. Garfield and the way she and Jack Malamud stare at each other once in a while as if they are waiting for a bomb to explode in their hands.

Now we follow Ms. Garfield and Jack M. downtown along the Bowery toward this supposedly terrific cheap restaurant he recommends near Chatham Square.

We pass right by Confucius.

Confucius stands about six feet high, and he looks like he knows everything you need to know in this life. I can tell it's Confucius even without looking at the inscription, because this afternoon I asked four different cabbies for any landmark in Chinatown near Mott Street and one of them said Confucius.

"You know, Trish, coming to New York is the best thing I ever did."

Hand in hand, Matt and I dodge through the honking cars that should be giving you the right of way but never do in New York.

"I didn't think you liked New York that much, Matt."

"I hate New York. That's why I'm glad I came, so I know once and for all never to live here. Look at those drivers—they don't care if they pulverize you!"

"Well, I happen to adore New York!"

"I think you're out of your mind," he says in a kindly tone.

"I think you don't have a mind to be out of," I answer in a kindly tone.

Before the argument has a chance to explode, we follow Ms. Garfield and Jack M. down a dozen stone steps into a basement restaurant called Hok Wok Hoo's. When the food arrives at our tables—sweet and sour chicken, bird's nest soup, steamed sea bass, etc.—Nadine proclaims with the air of an expert, "My mother cooks Chinese a lot. Everything gets shredded or cut bite-size and stir fried in a big steel wok."

She flashes me one of those sincere, let's-be-friends smiles she's been bestowing lately, which makes me so uncomfortable, I can't resist ribbing her.

"You know, Nadine, whenever I eat Chinese, I always have to go outside and take a *wok* in the fresh air."

Everybody groans at my rotten pun. I rise from my seat, trying to look as if I really am feeling under the weather.

Matt glares at me as I wiggle through the crowded chairs past Ms. Garfield's table. "I'll be right back, Ms. Garfield, just not feeling so well."

She nods to me, but her radar is tuned to Jack Malamud, warm, charming, teddy-bearish.

Once I'm up the steps to the sidewalk, I rush toward the statue of Confucius. Not getting killed crossing the Bowery traffic is an achievement. On the other side, a face appears from behind Confucius, the wonderful face of Zarkan Eleftherides, Jr.

"Am I late? I couldn't get away. Have you been here long? We didn't get to the restaurant when we planned. Have you eaten? I've been stuffing myself with—"

"Trisha?"

"Yes, Vic?"

"What's wrong?"

"Nothing."

"You sound like you got a bunch of problems bugging you."

I almost don't tell him the truth, but looking at his eyes in the neon light of the streetlamp, and thinking I might never see him again after I leave New York, I murmur, "I guess it gets me all nervous wanting so much to see you and then actually seeing you."

"Last night I had a dream, Trisha."

"A good dream?"

"I dreamed about you and me living happily ever after."

"Together or separately?"

Vic moves away from Confucius and instinctively I move with him, and then he moves back toward Confucius as if he is attached to the statue by an invisible thread.

"I can't stay long, Vic."

"I know."

"You don't mind?"

"Let's walk a little."

We walk beside each other for a few minutes without saying a word.

"There's a ring around the moon, Trisha!"

"It's green! I've never seen it green. Looks so cold."

"The moon ain't made of cheese, you know."

I giggle. "That's news."

"The moon is made of wishes and dreams. What are your dreams, Trisha?"

I turn my eyes up toward his face. His smooth brows give his face a hungry look because they contrast with the shadowy deep-set eyes and the hollows under his high cheekbones.

"I've got to get back, Vic."

"How does Confucius feel about kisses?"

"I hope he likes them."

"I'm going to kiss you."

He says it like he's waiting for an answer, but I don't say yes and I don't say no.

Slowly, Vic leans down toward me. I can almost feel his shadow like a soft living thing fall gently across my face, and then his lips press eagerly against mine.

Just his lips and my lips. No arms around each other or anything.

I want so much to feel something fabulous, but the kiss feels good, easy, nice, warm, cozy—definitely not fabulous.

"Ever since I arrived in New York," I say when our mouths part, "I can't get my mind unstuck from all the people. So many people and so many problems."

"Man, you wanna hook into people's problems, New York is the place. Me, I ain't gonna get dragged under. I'm gonna fly!"

"But problems are real, Vic. Like with us—there's Matt, and there's my going back to Cleveland only days from now, before you and I can really . . ."

"Before we can really what?"

There isn't any answer I can give him.

"I figure"—he creases his forehead—"we ought to know each other at least forever."

His hands close around my arms—the strength in his fingers surprises me—and then his hands are gone and he's turning the corner and I'm alone.

15

APRIL SNOW. THE city wakes with a shock of snow. Night snow falling while we slept. Sidewalks all vanilla ice cream.

I remember Vic's kiss.

What was missing?

All day Matt is especially sweet to me, opening doors for me, buying me things, as if instinctively he realizes part of me is being pulled away from him and he wants to get me back. Matt really acts kind. Until we have that awful argument.

Vic promised to tell me about himself, answer all my questions, but last night in Chinatown he didn't answer a thing. I should have asked him. But we had so little time.

How can the weather have changed so suddenly? When I get out of bed the windowpane feels like a sheet of ice. The sky sparkles clean, the sun licks the white rooftops. Think of all those people getting out of bed and touching their windowpanes. Maybe Manhattan is the wrong place for me. I don't like worrying about all those people you bump into and get to know just a little edge of, just enough to make you think about them too much. I'm too young to worry about other people's problems. I just want to have a swell time. But what *about* Eleanor Roosevelt—will she find her lost husband? Will Peter Parker's wife let him visit his little daughter? Will the bellhop ever win enough money gambling to start a shoe store? And the bag lady outside the coffee shop every morning. Will she be that way forever, day in, day out, for years to come? I shudder, feeling more and more depressed.

Nadine is snoring, hardly a snore really, just a flutter. Last night when I got back from Vic and Confucius, she and Matt were digging into dessert together.

Usually, more often than not, when Matt kisses me, my body starts galloping inside, sort of like horses slow-motion leaping in the surf, and my mind starts seeing a nice house, a backyard, kids, a bedroom set, two cars, vacations every summer, friends for dinner, a good life like my parents—but something missing like a piece of a jigsaw puzzle.

When Vic kissed me last night it was like the kiss wasn't physical; the kiss was something new to me, not exciting like Matt's, no gallops or anything, more like a fragment of Vic and a fragment of me being glad to be together.

Anyway, the most important thing about today—apart from the snow and the Guggenheim Museum and the Fashion Institute of Technology—is that Matt is a real hero when Toni gets pickpocketed.

Actually she only thinks she gets pickpocketed. We are trooping out of the Guggenheim on Fifth Avenue and 89th Street, opposite Central Park, and Toni has just paid for a book she liked in the museum bookstore with some of her traveler's checks. In the museum, Ms. Garfield tried hard to conceal how proud she was when we came upon a painting by Jack Malamud, more of his weird feet in acrylics on a canvas the size of your living room, and all of us made noises like we were real impressed, which we were. Then, on the slushy sidewalk—and we aren't exactly dressed for the unexpected wet cold—a nasty-looking young guy in a down jacket bumps into Toni and bounces away downtown. Instinctively, she digs her hand into the pocket of her spring coat.

"Help!" she shouts. "He took my traveler's checks! Stop him."

What impresses me about Matt is that he doesn't waste a minute, but sprints forward after the vicious-looking guy, who is pretty huge, but who looks back with a scared expression nonetheless when he hears Toni shouting. Zigzagging, the guy shoots through the Fifth Avenue traffic and leaps the stone wall bordering the park—with Matt in hot pursuit.

"Oh, no!" Toni moans. She's found the traveler's checks in her *other* pocket. "He didn't steal it!"

"Matt, wait!" I yell, but he can't hear me over the noise of traffic. I burst away from our group—visions of the guy in the down jacket pulling a knife on Matt or something—and nearly get hit twice by cabs as I race toward the park.

"Matt! Matt!"

I scramble over the wall.

"Hi." Matt hiccups below me.

He's lying flat on his back in the snow, on the other side of the wall, his embarrassed crooked grin showing perfect white teeth.

"Slipped," he explains, jacking to his feet, then shaking the dust of snow off his hair and clothes.

"Toni found her traveler's checks, Matt."

"Well, isn't that nice," he grunts, slapping snow off his pants.

"You look very interesting with snow on your hair."

His eyes catch mine. "Think so?"

"You'll be very handsome when you're sixty-five and your hair is all white."

He walks his fingertips along my forearm and up over my shoulder and strokes the back of my neck.

"What are you doing?"

"Touching your neck."

"That makes me uncomfortable, Matt."

"What's wrong with touching your neck, for crying out loud?!"

"I don't know. Maybe it's being out here on the street."

His face darkens, stiffly. "Yeah!" he blurts explosively.

I keep my mouth shut for once, which short circuits a fight for the moment. A few minutes later we are on a bus crosstown through the park, and even though it annoys me that lately whenever I want to talk, he wants us to be touching, still I have this good feeling too, because the way he took off after Toni's "stolen" checks makes you know you are pretty protected when you are with a boy like Matt.

But lately we're so sarcastic to each other, I hate it. Which is what happens after we all transfer to the downtown Seventh Avenue bus heading toward F.I.T.

"What are you reading?" Matt asks, turning around suddenly across the aisle.

The bus is so crowded we had to sit separately, each of us with a stranger, and since there are so many people jammed in I don't think Matt is going to notice me reading three pieces of paper that were left for me in my box at the hotel this morning. Maybe I'm setting it up for Matt to be jealous and curious, but I don't think so. I just feel good reading what's on those three pieces of paper.

So Matt says, "What are you reading?" Like making conversation.

"Nothing," I say, folding away the pieces of paper as if they're of no importance.

"How can you read nothing?" he throws at me.

"How many more stops before we get off?" I ask Matt pleasantly.

"How can you read nothing?" his voice grates.

"What are you, the district attorney?" I slash back at Matt.

"You know, Trish." Matt's voice suddenly gets all sweet cream and butter. "I think arguments are really healthy between men and women. I bet they're very useful for preventing marriage." He laughs at his own dumb joke.

"You know, Matt," I reply in my most genteel manner, "anybody ever tell you you'd make a perfect stranger?"

Fortunately we arrive at the Fashion Institute of Technology. I guess we both have time to realize that we're arguing for no good reason and that we'd really rather be nice to each other. So we sit together in the F.I.T. auditorium and watch this fabulous student fashion show, but I have to admit that I grab the first chance I get, when I'm alone in the ladies room, to read each of the three notes that were left for me.

The first note says: "I'll be waiting on the Staten Island ferry, any time after eleven."

The third note says: "The mice are chewing the root."

The second note says: "Did the earth move when I kissed you? No? I'll have it fixed right away."

16

IT'S TWELVE MINUTES to eleven. The cabbie whips me downtown, yakking all the way, doesn't let me get a word in edgewise. I lean back into the vinyl seat. The city feels like a huge empty labyrinth, here and there a splash of light, a neon bar, a few pedestrians, traffic signals, the World Trade Center two faraway cliffs getting bigger and bigger, the Wall Street office buildings closing in over the narrow streets, dark Trinity Church like a black elephant caught between the high canyon walls.

A few minutes ago I snuck out of the Hotel Manhattan. Not even seen by Peter Parker, hunched at the front desk. Ms. Garfield had insisted—and checked—that everyone hit the hay early. When I was sure the others were asleep, I threw on jeans, a sweater, my sneakers, my warmest jacket, and slipped out.

If anyone discovers I'm not there I'll explain I had insomnia and went for a walk. Oh, sure!

Battery Park and the Staten Island ferry building loom ahead.

"Is the tip alright?" The meter reads six dollars; I'm holding out seven.

He fists my money with a sigh. "Honey, if they drop

the Bomb tonight, only me an' you an' God are gonna know if dis is an okay tip, see?"

Up the marble stairs, a quarter in the turnstile, scattered people down at the loading area on long highbacked wooden benches. Where's Vic?

Two young guys, quarter-inch crewcuts and forearm tattoos, stare at me. A needle of fear quivers in my ribs. I'm alone. A girl alone. Late night. New York. A hoarse voice blares over a loudspeaker and a moment later a light blinks over the middle loading door: *Ferry Arriving.* The forearm tattoos are wearing high-heeled cowboy boots which click-click-click in my direction, then stop as if they hit an invisible wall. Two hands from behind me cover my eyes.

"Guess who?"

"Vic!"

"And who else is with me?"

"Nobody."

"Someone's with me, Trisha."

"Is it a friend of yours?"

"Definitely."

"I don't know your friends."

"Take a guess!"

"I can't . . . wait! I know who's with you—it's Charlie Chaplin!"

His hands fall away from my face. I whirl around.

"You're alone."

"Are you sure, Trisha?"

One moment his eyes are so intense they nearly scare me, then suddenly the fierceness melts and a smile sparkles.

"Even when I'm alone, I'm not alone. I've got my friends. And now I've got you."

He looks so different without makeup or disguises. It's the first time I've seen him just natural. I notice how his bristly eyebrows arch over his eyes. I notice how his nostrils flare when he smiles. I notice the long wavy gold

hair with sparks of fire, the wide brow, the chin that
sticks out and emphasizes the changeability of his mouth,
and his eyes, exciting gray-blue eyes—his eyes are different from any I've ever seen. Most people's eyes get
wide with excitement, but his look almost closed and
sleepy at those times, and then when he's very calm his
eyes go wide open.

"You're staring at me like you've seen a ghost."

"I didn't realize, Vic."

"No, I like it when you stare. Hey, quick! We'll miss
the ferry!"

We skitter on board just before the chains go clanking
away and the ferry gets unlocked from its mooring.

Did anyone but me ever go back and forth on the
Staten Island ferry twelve times from midnight till the
first sunlight makes the East River look like blue milk?

All night the running lights of the ferry make the foam
that washes past the bow of the boat appear almost like
phosphorous, alive.

I'll never forget as long as I live the stars over the
Brooklyn Bridge like icy ornaments on a Christmas tree
the size of the sky.

Can you believe the seagulls don't sleep all night?
We keep throwing them peanuts and popcorn over the
stern of the boat, watching their wings as they dive into
the luminous green-white wake that ribbons behind us.

We also give names to our favorite seagulls. Vic names
his Seamus Vittorio Aristotle Rappaport McDonald, because he says he himself is part-Irish, Italian, Greek,
Jewish, and Scottish.

I christen my bird Miracle.

"Why Miracle?"

I shrug my shoulders.

All night we tell each other everything there is to tell.
Our whole lives.

I even tell him about the total of 24,000 chocolate M
& M's I sold to the relatives, friends, neighbors, and

storekeepers I could persuade to help me raise money for the trip to Manhattan.

And I tell him how Matt and I first met as freshmen at Patrick Henry. How my father is a dentist and my mother started her own catering business from scratch and I'm an only child and how I've dreamed of a career in New York ever since my first art class with Ms. Garfield. I tell him little things I can remember from my childhood I think will interest him like how I cried for a month when the parakeet I named Uncle Bill that happened to fly into our window and we kept for ten months got out of his cage and the window and never came back.

And Vic tells me his story.

My life story sounds so comfortable and protected in comparison with his.

"My old man I hear from twice a year; he's always on the move. Mom divorced him when I was two. He's a drunk, has liver trouble, gambles, always broke. Sometimes I send him a few bucks. Mom, though, she's the greatest! But she's always getting divorced. Can't stand being single. The latest husband is only five years older than me, can you believe it? Works in a radio station, Chicago, so Mom's out there with him, sends me dough to live on when she can, and I stay here in her apartment. New York is where you make it."

He tells me little things too, like growing up mostly in the street, stealing, gang fights, his life changing when he "went absolutely *ape* over magic tricks and then I saw Marcel Marceau doing pantomime, and I knew pantomime was *it* for me. But making a living in pantomime is worse than being an actor, so I figure I'll try acting, commercials, soaps, anything. I'm not proud."

He also tells me about his three best friends—Kiku, Fish, and Efren—who are also from broken homes, and seniors with him in the High School of Performing Arts.

"Hey, we are really family to each other. You've got to meet them, Trisha."

Our arms are touching as we lean on the wooden rail of the ferry. The sky brightens, the stars fade. The tip of Manhattan looks like a forest of glass and metal as the engines push us closer. North of us the lights go out on the Brooklyn Bridge. The pilings ahead are scarred, splintered, black with tar. The engines reverse, water churning and foaming at the hull, then stop, and the steel rim of the ferry glides into creaking contact with the pilings, and the boat lurches. I find myself in Vic's arms.

"I love you, Trisha."

"You can't."

"Why not?"

"We've seen each other—how many—four times?"

"So what?"

"I don't want to be unhappy, Vic."

"Hey, what's unhappy about 'I love you?'"

"It scares me."

His eyes are soft, yearning. I want him to kiss me. I turn my face upward. I can hear the sailors locking the rim of the ferry into its moorings, people moving past us to get off, but I don't care. Please kiss me, Vic. I know he wants me to say I love him, but I can't. Not yet. He seems to know what I'm thinking. His lips graze the corner of my mouth so lightly and move slowly like the touch of a feather across my lips and then press down hard for a moment. We hold each other. He needs me more than he can express, I can sense it. For the first time in my life someone needs me the way you read about, and I feel as if I'm getting swept away.

"I'll take you back," he murmurs as we leave the boat and sailors and water and seagulls and the river and the last stars behind us.

"I'd better go, yes."

I feel he needs me not only as his girl, the way Matt does, but also as something more—like he needs everything I am, everything I can be. I don't know how else to say it. Does that make sense? Sounds phony when I put it into words. Maybe it's some kind of maternal instinct.

Or maybe I'm fooling myself. Isn't it possibly the stealth and the danger of getting found out that make it all so romantic with Vic? Or just that we both know the time we have together is so short, just days?

"Don't forget."

"What, Vic?"

The subway roars us uptown from Battery Park. Even this early men and women are going to work, yawning and reading newspapers.

"What I told you."

He leaves me a few yards from the hotel steps with a touch of his fingers to his lips and the curl of a smile that could mean a million different things.

The bag lady, huddled in a corner, looks asleep, but as I pass her I see one eye slide open to watch me.

Somewhere over Manhattan there's a pigeon named Miracle and another named Seamus Vittorio Aristotle Rappaport McDonald.

17

"WHERE'VE YOU BEEN?"

The voice is Matt's but the face is different than I've ever seen him. He was pacing back and forth in the lobby when I swung inside from the street. Now he stares at me as if I were a stranger.

"Where've you been, Trisha?"

"Out."

"Just *out*?"

"That's right."

"Any idea what time it is?"

"Matt, you're not my father."

He looks so unhappy, I hate being the cause. I don't want to lie, but I also don't want to tell the truth.

"Matt, can't we just leave it that I wasn't here for a while, and not make an issue of it?"

The muscles in his jaw twitch and his lips tighten. "I was feeling rotten, Trisha, about how much you and I keep arguing lately. Couldn't sleep. Finally had to talk to you. I knocked on your door. Ruth woke up, said you're not in bed. I've been sitting here waiting for the last five hours."

"I didn't realize."

"So what did you do while you were out? Walk around

the block? Bet you can go around a lot of times in five hours. You must be really dizzy, Trisha."

"I hate it when you're sarcastic."

"I suppose you're never sarcastic?"

"Okay, let's drop it, Matt."

"Do you admit it sounds peculiar when you say you've been outside five hours on the streets of New York doing nothing."

"I didn't say I was doing nothing."

"What *were* you doing, Trisha?"

"I was on the Staten Island ferry."

"You were on the Staten Island ferry? All night? What do you do on the Staten Island ferry all night?"

"Feed the seagulls."

"I don't believe you!"

I raise my right hand as if I am a witness being sworn in: "I swear to tell the truth, the half-truth, and nothing but the truth."

Matt sticks his jaw out aggressively. "Listen, Trisha, if you were in my shoes, you'd be steaming too!"

"I don't demand to know everything *you* do when we're not together."

"I'm asking, not demanding. You'd ask me if I went wandering around Manhattan alone in the middle of the night."

"Why are you so bothered? Be honest, Matt, it can't just be me."

He hesitates, rubbing a knuckle into his chin. I long to reach out and touch his hair and tell him how confused I am, how lucky I feel sometimes to be his girl, because even though he doesn't say I love you, he cares, I know he cares. And yet there's Vic, Vic's presence lingering with me. I love you, Trisha. You can't love me, Vic. Vic touches a darkness in my chest, a darkness whirling with stars.

"I—I didn't tell you"—Matt's voice sounds unsteady—"I got in touch with my brother."

"The one in Vermont your parents don't talk to?"

Matt's face hardens, his voice bitter. "He's living in New York now. I phoned him. Says he's too busy to see me this week, but maybe the next time I'm in New York. *Too busy! Maybe the next time!*"

"So forget it, Matt. Anyway, you told me you hated your brother for always beating you up."

"I never said *hated*. I said *angry*." His eyes are storming at me. "All I wanted to know was what you were doing out all night, and you get me going about my selfish, rotten brother! WHO WERE YOU OUT WITH ALL NIGHT, TRISHA?"

Matt's raised voice brings Peter Parker walking quickly toward us from the hotel desk, obviously to try and avoid a loud argument in the lobby. I hustle out the hotel entrance and down the steps.

Matt follows me, chin jerking belligerently. "I want to know who, Trisha! Where you went and why! Or else let's just say we're not going steady as of right now!"

The bag lady is standing near the curb. Sunlight is streaming over the rooftops and all the snow has melted. Steam seems to be rising from the manholes. It's April again. The bag lady is younger than I thought. No gray, just thick black straight hair, and she's pulling a comb through the tangles.

"I mean it, Trisha!"

The bag lady has a very sturdy figure. I'm glad the weather is warmer for her.

"I'm sorry, Matt."

An orange appears in the bag lady's hand. Delicately, very precisely, her fingers peel away its skin, while she drops each torn orange fragment into the pocket of her dark, ankle-length dress.

"Okay, if that's the way you want it, Trisha."

18

WHAT AM I doing on the back of a moped, bumping along at seventeen miles per hour in downtown traffic on Second Avenue—a girl could get killed the way these busdrivers and vans go swishing past with inches to spare—and I cling more tightly to Vic, who swings the handlebars of the borrowed motorbike from side to side and keeps up a barrage of comments as if the other drivers could hear him.

"Oh, that's beautiful, don't even signal! Stay in your lane, dummy! Very smart, man, your brains must be disconnected. Go ahead, keep honking, just what New York needs, a little more noise. Give that driver ten silver dollars for Meatball of the Month!"

He laughs, and his ribs pass the vibration of his laughter into my forearms.

It's like living in a dream, a dream about the two of us, only it's real. Riding through Manhattan, hair blowing in the warm April afternoon air, passing car radios offering a moment of rock or jazz or Sinatra, police sirens, a silver helicopter racketing over the street, hear air hammers chopping apart a sidewalk, two blocks later the smell of fresh tar poured on the potholes and steamrollered, then a spidery crane twenty stories high lifts a naked steel girder to be riveted on top of a rising building; it's dizzying and upsetting and wonderful to see, with my body tight against Vic's . . . it's almost heaven except for the thoughts I shouldn't be thinking.

"Tell me their names again, Vic, will you?"

The airstream gives his voice a rugged sound. "Kiku, she's a music major, you and she will be *tight*, believe me. And Efren, he's into dance, beautiful dude. And Fish, he's a genius, theater major, he's a little off the wall but if you're his friend he'll cut his arm off for you."

South of Fourteenth Street, Second Avenue begins to look more like Greenwich Village, with theaters, a church, coffee shops, boutiques, antiques, but also a lot of side streets that look pretty raggedy.

Matt keeps popping unhappily into my happiness, and I feel completely cut off from him and furious that he broke us up the way he did this morning, although he had a perfect right to, I guess.

He and the rest of the kids are probably gaping around the offices of *Vogue* magazine right this minute, according to Ms. Garfield's schedule, and I'm sorry I'm missing a place that must be so drenched in glamour, but I'm not sorry either because I'm here with Vic. I was so wiped out this morning, no sleep, the fight with Matt, that I told Ms. Garfield I was feeling sick.

"You do look exhausted, Trisha," Ms. Garfield said.

"Kind of headachy and my stomach feels like it's in my shoes."

"May be a one-day flu. Stay in bed today."

I sighed. "Sounds good. Oh, Ms. G., I hear Mr. Malamud got us all theater tickets. Must've cost a fortune."

Ms. G. looked like she just bit into a lemon. "Yes, he's been very . . . uh, kind."

The way she said *kind* seemed to mean something she wasn't really saying.

I didn't feel bad about saying I felt headachy and sick, because I wasn't exactly lying—just exaggerating.

Also I knew that if Vic called I'd be up and out of bed like a shot. When I climbed wearily into bed, maybe groaning a little to exaggerate my symptoms, the only one who knew I'd been out all night was Ruth.

"Did you talk to Matt?" she asked pointedly. Toni was already in the lobby gushing over Peter Parker, and Nadine was singing off-key in the shower.

"We decided not to go steady anymore."

She was shocked. "We?"

"Me."

"What happened?"

"We're always arguing."

"Is that all?"

"I don't want to talk about it, Ruth."

"I'm worried about you."

I patted her hand comfortingly. "If you want to worry, worry about Toni. I saw her downstairs with Peter Parker again."

A sadness seemed to envelop her, like a windshield when it gets all fogged up. I felt a burst of impatience, impatience with all my friends—they seemed so predictable, they seemed like they were dragging me back to Cleveland.

That's why, even though I only had four hours sleep, when Vic called me at the hotel my heart zoomed up through the ceiling.

So now a right turn on Fourth Street and we slow to a stop in front of a crummy red-brick tenement in between two even crummier tenements, although across the street there's a disco with a futuristic aluminum design.

"That's it." Vic stabs a finger left of the tenement hallway toward a huge plate-glass storefront smeared with whitewash and with a crack like a jagged lightning bolt from top to bottom. Above the plate-glass window a peeling green sign says BODEGA. Rusty garbage cans spill over onto the sidewalk.

I don't see much of the slick New York rhythm in this place.

Except for a girl and two guys in paint-splattered overalls who stroll out of the closed bodega with brushes and paint-rollers, waving hello to us.

Vic's friends are just exactly the New York I'm falling in love with.

The girl is Kiku, small, delicate bones, Eurasian face, transparent skin, a quiet, firm voice full of musical ups and downs, and you sense the way she holds the handle of her paint-roller there's an energy in her that is Manhattan all the way.

And she is blind.

She extends her hand when we meet, palm up, fingers open, waiting for my hand to touch hers. She doesn't say much until I've been given a white painter's hat to protect my hair, and overalls, and after several hours of slapping fresh paint over the discolored walls of the store I'm fascinated by how she manages not to make a mess with her long-handled paint-roller. That's when she asks, "Do you like me, Trisha?"

I can't help laughing. "Yes, I do."

"Why are you laughing?"

"I guess because I don't have the guts to ask anybody so honestly if they like me."

Her seeing-eye dog, a black Labrador, lies curled near her.

And one of the guys, when Vic first introduces us, takes my hand, like a Spanish aristocrat, and bows. "I am Efren Velasquez Medina Duarte Gomez."

Efren is handsome, a sort of Latin Robert Redford, tall, suave, restless, even when he's standing still he looks like he's dancing, and when he lays down his brush for a rest, his long elegant hands fold and refold these futuristic paper planes that glide silently across the store space to crash softly into our backs. One lands on my head. We laugh.

Then there is Fish. His real name is Nicholas Kaufman. He calls himself Fish because his mother always tried to get him to eat fish and he hated it.

"I dig the name Fish because it's so illogical to me, you get it?"

He's always bopping, snapping his fingers, reeling off the kind of jazzy poetic street talk that's nearly impossible to imitate.

"That's real bad, man. What'd you say? Yo, mama!"

Fish is short, thick-chested, with sinewy arms and neck from lifting weights, and he often breaks his painting to do pushups or press up into a handstand, but when he sprinkles theater talk around, you listen hard.

"I think the audience sometimes needs to know exactly what will happen next, so it can relax and really get *into* it. Other times the audience needs to be kept guessing."

I can see from how proud Vic is when he introduces me to each of his friends that they *are* his family, like he said.

"Floor needs sanding and polishing," Vic announces when we are finally soaking the brushes and rollers in turpentine, "but this is gonna be one hell of our own little cabaret theater."

"Just pray we can scrape up the scratch to pay the nut on this place."

"We *will*." Kiku glows. "Because we don't just want to make money, we want people who come here to feel like they have friends who care."

"When I dance, even my father, the famous San Juan surgeon, will sit here one day and think how happy he is that his crazy son Efren did not go to medical school!"

"Let's hold hands and feel the energy," Kiku proposes.

We make a circle on the scarred wood floor in the middle of the battered old store, which looks so hopefully theatrical with its fresh coat of dark blue-gray paint, and we hold hands, close our eyes, sitting crosslegged, the sharp smell of wet paint surrounding us, and Kiku speaks quietly, "Let the energy flow from inside you, the energy of love, the energy of the universe, take the energy as it comes to you, and give the energy away àt the same time."

I've got to admit, sitting there with one hand in Vic's hand, the other in Kiku's, that I feel like they are into stuff that is really too far out for me. Yet at the same time there is a closeness I'm hungry for, but I can't really let myself go a hundred percent, not with a whole future to decide and a whole past to worry about.

And later, outside on the street, Kiku takes me aside before I mount up on the moped with Vic, and she whispers, "I've never seen Vic so happy and so hopeful."

Which is a weird thing for a blind person to say— she's never *seen* him so happy. I feel a little resentful, her saying it, because I don't want to be made responsible for hurting him when I have to go back to Cleveland.

But when I've said goodbye to Kiku and to Fish and Efren, and I'm holding Vic tight on the swerving moped, a thought sneaks in for the first time that maybe Vic and his friends and his world aren't just a flash in the pan for me, a ten-day taste of romance.

Maybe there could be more.

19

SOMEONE IS WEEPING in the room next door, a thin scratchy voice. It can't be the waitress, Eleanor Roosevelt. I clearly remember her voice as being deep and fluid. But it is her room.

I'm standing in the hallway, about to twist the hotel key in our door, listening to the high-pitched sobbing. Any minute Ms. Garfield and the Cleveland crew will be rampaging back from their afternoon visit to a fashionable clothes manufacturer on Seventh Avenue, where they were to see every phase of the business, from the designer's drawing board to the modeling in the showroom for women rich enough to pay a thousand dollars per dress.

I sure better be in bed when they get here.

But if it isn't Eleanor Roosevelt crying, who is it? Maybe she moved out, gave up looking for her husband. Maybe there's some other woman moved in, crying over a completely different problem. Maybe I should knock on the door and ask if the person needs help.

Mind your own business, Trisha. This is New York. People don't want strangers interfering, even next-door strangers.

Well, New York or not, I'm Trisha Sargent and I can't let somebody cry like that without trying to help. So I knock—lightly—on the door.

"Go away! Get lost! You bum! You . . . you . . . I never want to see you again!"

Now the voice is definitely Eleanor Roosevelt. I guess when she cries her voice gets thin and scratchy.

It's a good thing she doesn't want help, because I'm hardly inside our room, my nightgown on, jumping into bed, when a rap at the door and a familiar voice hurry me under the covers.

"It's Ms. Garfield, Trisha. Can I come in?"

"Sure!"

Ms. Garfield enters wearing a very chic velvet pants suit and a leather jacket, with her hair done in a dramatic manner.

"Feeling better?" She eases down on the edge of my bed and pats my knee.

"Much."

She is trying very hard to concentrate her attention on me, but I can tell her mind is off in some other place. Jack Malamud?

"Do any new sketches?"

"Not yet. I'll do them tonight."

"Your drawings, Trisha, have changed since we came here."

"How?"

"Not so superficial, not so slick. More . . . connected to feelings."

My cheeks get hot with embarrassment.

"I think I envy you, Trisha."

"Why?"

"You're at the beginning of things."

Her eyes, green eyes usually so electric, seem dimmer, and her hands, usually shaping the air in a thousand interesting forms, lay motionless in her lap. "Do you know Robert Frost? 'Two roads diverged in a wood.'"

"Oh, I love that poem. We had to memorize it.

"'Two roads diverged in a wood, and I—
   I took the one less traveled by,
   And that has made all the difference.'"

"Myself," she says flatly, "I took the one *more* traveled by."

"Are you glad?"

"Not always." She stands up, straightens her shoulders, and throws off whatever was glooming her, as if it were a coat too heavy for the weather. "Shall I bring you dinner or do you feel well enough to eat Greek food with us across the street?"

The Greek restaurant Ms. G. meant is not actually across the street from our hotel but down the block at the corner of Sixth Avenue, and when we arrive—I've decided I feel well enough to eat out—we have to wait for a table. Only half our group is here; the rest, including Matt and Nadine—she was so conspicuously clinging to his arm—divided up into twos and threes to eat at other nearby restaurants. As far as I know, only Toni decided to remain in the hotel, where I suspect she might be meeting Peter Parker.

Nobody has the courage to order the octopus, but the table soon fills up with souvlaki and mousaka and crumbly white feta cheese in salad. It's probably the last expensive meal any of us will be able to afford, because we are all way down in the money department. Tomorrow we'll be at the sharing-hamburgers stage.

"I hate seeing Matt with Nadine that way," Ruth drops, in between sips of soup.

"I hope they have a good time." Well, don't I? Who are you kidding, Trisha? The souvlaki on my fork might as well be broiled Kleenex because I'm so preoccupied with the image of Matt and Nadine kissing that my taste buds must be in a state of rigor mortis. When he kisses her, will she react the way I do? Will he feel her trembling against him? Will he like her lips and her body better than mine?

For a moment I feel my insides falling away below me. I remember how Matt can make me shiver with waves of excitement through my body. Most girls would probably say don't let a guy who really turns you on slip through your fingers.

But most girls haven't met a Vic Uris. Or a Kiku, an Efren, a Nick the Fish.

"How was the visit to *Vogue* this morning?" I ask Ruth, to make conversation and get away from my own confusion. She's been quiet, absorbed in her plate, stabbing at her food and chewing each bite as if it were her last, all of which I know means Herman Katzenellenbogen.

"It was okay. Swell offices. Everybody who works there must spend a fortune for clothes. I mean a *fortune*. Would you like some of my feta cheese, Trisha? I don't think I'm hungry."

When Ruth isn't hungry I know the world is coming to an end.

"Herman problems?"

"This trip is turning into a disaster," Ruth mumbles. "I can't believe you and Matt broke up. I can't believe it. I cannot believe it."

"Did you call Herman?"

"Every time I phone him his mother says he's out. I couldn't get him all day yesterday and today. Every single time. 'He's out, operator,' she says. What do you think it means, Trisha?"

"I think it means he's out. Did you leave a message for him to call back?"

"No. I always call person-to-person. I tried last night

right up to ten-thirty. I mean I *tried*. Ten-thirty he's not home. That's got to tell you something. And he hasn't called me."

"Ruth, Herman loves you."

"That's the trouble."

"Huh?"

"He says he loves me, but he can't *really* love me, because if he really knew me, he'd feel the way I do about me, which is just plain *yuck*!"

"Don't you know how attractive you are?"

"Please don't lie to me, Trisha!" Ruth stuffs a hunk of souvlaki in her mouth and chews away furiously, her oval face so pale under the black bangs, her eyes obviously blinking away tears.

I give up! I mean, Ruth *is* attractive. I've heard so many girls envy her wide beautifully boned shoulders and large breasts and slender waist and tiny feet. She's crazy. We're all crazy. I mean, why can't we just feel good right *now* instead of always groping to make things better?

Anyway, the waiter is writing down our orders for dessert when Toni appears hurrying into the restaurant. She catches my eye and heads straight for me. Her face tells me there is trouble.

"You've got to call Cleveland, Trisha. Your folks are okay, but they want you to call them right away."

I hurry outside with Toni, after explaining to Ms. Garfield, who is eating at a different table.

On the street, Toni hooks my arm and hurries me toward the hotel. "It's not Cleveland or your folks. I made that up. It's Matt and Nadine. We've got to do something before Ms. Garfield gets back."

"What's wrong?"

"You better see for yourself."

The smell, when I open the door to our hotel room, Toni at my back, the *smell* almost drives me right back into the hallway. It doesn't take a genius to figure out that someone's celebrating something.

Matt doesn't even glance at us. Wobbly, giggling, pursing his lips and trying unsuccessfully to whistle, he has hold of Nadine's wrists and is pulling her—she's groaning and moaning—along the carpet toward the bathroom. Nadine's face looks green and clammy.

I force myself not to say it's disgusting. Not to say it's stupid. Not to say it's thoughtless, dangerous, ugly.

"Matt, we've got to get you back in your room before Ms. Garfield gets back."

He drops Nadine's wrists with a thud. "Well hello-o-o! Glad to see you, Trish. Nadine, say hello to Trish."

Nadine lies there glassy-eyed and sick-looking.

"Nadine's shy," Matt whispers slyly in that silly voice. "I thought I better get her to the bathroom before she gets sick."

"I'll put Nadine in the shower," I say to Toni in my best take-charge manner. "You get Matt back to his room."

"Okay," Toni agrees. She catches Matt's wrist. "Come on, pumpkin. We'll get you sober, right now!"

"Unhand me, woman!" He yanks away from Toni. He belches, looks around as if somebody else were to blame and points in my direction: "She's my nurse. Trisha's my nurse. Come on, nurse!"

I nod to Toni. She drops Matt's wrist and starts working on Nadine. I lead Matt by the arm, out the door and down the hallway to the elevator.

Stewing inside with all kinds of contradictory feelings, I don't know whether to kick him or comfort him. I even feel just a smidgin of stupid pride that I was the one who drove him to this.

"Do you believe in being dumb to kind animals?" Matt's voice sounds so young, he smiles so innocently and helplessly, that an urge comes over me to hold his hand and be like kids together, just running back home where it's safe and everybody knows us.

"You look very familiar," he murmurs to me as the elevator door closes us inside. "You have a twin sister in Cleveland?" Then he turns green, holding his stomach and his mouth as the elevator drops to his floor.

I rush him into his room. He stumbles toward the bathroom. I shove him into the bathtub, swivel the knob to cold, and watch him sputter under the blast of water.

"Hey, I'm drowning!" He moves to get out from under the shower but I shove him back.

"You're on the swim team, swim yourself sober!"

His big fingers lock closed around my wrist. He hauls me into the shower with him.

"You rat! You crumb! Let me go, you big clown!"

He's cracking up, laughing, splitting his sides.

I never hit anybody in my life. I don't think I ever even made a fist before. But now it happens—I'm gasping under the shower and my fist all by itself crashes into Matt's nose.

"You macho dingbat!" I shout at the top of my voice, leaping out of the bathtub.

The last thing I see of him is the shower ricocheting off his head, blood running from his nose, and a big watermelon grin slicing his face as he laughs uproariously.

20

FOUR MORE DAYS. Only four days left. Don't think about it, Trisha!

I can't think about anything but.

Vic phones and asks to meet my friends, including Matt. I want to refuse but he persuades me by saying: "Suppose I never see you again? Your friends are part of you. They'll help me remember us. I'll see you tonight at the Ambassador Theater. You afraid your friends will be able to tell I'm in love with you?"

The day of our Broadway play, Ms. Garfield really keeps us on the go—I've never seen her so animated and so tense—from the Frick Museum in the morning to a small graphic arts advertising business after lunch and another visit to the Museum of Modern Art. Personally I'm glad we're so busy because it keeps me from worrying about Vic meeting Matt.

After a cheap dinner—nearly everybody's broke, and the current phrase among us for meals is "Diet time!"—we foot it downtown to Forty-fifth near Schubert Alley, more theaters than I've ever imagined on one street, and waiting outside under the marquee with a pocketful of tickets is twinkling chunky Jack Malamud.

Ms. G. touches her mouth to Mr. M's, and all of us except me murmur approvingly, "That's the way, Ms. G! Go for it! Okay! All *right*!"

My reaction is more sour. Don't ask me why, but I sense that Mr. M. might make Ms. G. very unhappy.

And then, right there on the edge of the sidewalk, while cabs and limousines and a horse and carriage deposit arriving theatergoers, I hear the sound of a loud music box playing a tinkly waltz, and whom do I see but my Charlie Chaplin boy.

Floppy black pants, tight black suit jacket, oversize black shoes, black mustache on white greasepainted skin, cane in hand, body articulating exactly like a mechanical wind-up figure to the beat of the tinkly waltz—Vic! It's Vic, of course.

What's sad is that only a handful of people take notice of his act and contribute a few coins when he holds out his black derby.

But he knows, and I know, that he's really doing his act for us. I'm nervous as a cat, wondering how he's going to manage to introduce himself to my friends and me in some casual way, as if we are meeting each other for the first time, but I'm ready for anything. It's exciting; we're like conspirators.

Equally exciting is the growing crowd outside the bright theater, the sparkling marquee, the huge photos of the actors, the sense of people filled with anticipation, the colorful medley of clothing from casual to practically operatic.

The only fly in the ointment is the twinge I feel when Matt and Nadine hang out arm in arm, all whispers and touches, as if they were the only two people in the world. You *know* he's out to punish me—no one switches affection so fast—or do they?

Anyway, soon we're sweeping into the orchestra of the theater, plush red seats, fat naked baby cupids and winged lady angels painted on the ceiling in a blue sky.

It's painful watching Marcia Carter trying to maneuver herself into a seat near Fat Jack, and failing, and Toni maneuvering herself *out* of a seat next to Teddy Jackson's pompadour, which looks higher and oilier than ever. People!

And watching Ms. G. with Jack Malamud. I cannot figure her out, she's so *up*, hands dancing, neon green eyes flashing, after the usher parks us in our center-row seats.

I can't believe Ms. G. is the same woman I saw this morning when I went to her room with two days worth of overdue sketches in my hand. I was about to knock on her door when I heard the sound of glass shattering. Then silence. Then more glass, this time exploding against the door. Silence. I waited, listening. I considered leaving. Curiosity got the better of me. I knocked.

"Ms. Garfield? It's Trisha."

I heard glass being swept up and dropped into something metallic.

The door opened. Ms. Garfield smiled moodily, raking a few strands of hair back into place behind her ear.

"Yes, Trisha?"

"My overdue sketches."

"Good. Everything all right?"

"With me? Oh, sure!"

"I understand that you and Matt are . . ."

"Yes."

"Unhappy?"

"Not yet."

She laughed kind of grimly. Then I think she realized I could see the smashed mirror over her shoulder.

"Sometimes it's difficult to understand why we get ourselves into situations that . . ." For a moment I imagined she was on the verge of revealing to me something very personal about herself and Jack Malamud.

Instead, she clapped her hands together smartly, as if to chase away her own ill-humor. "Well! We'd better get ready! Busy schedule today!"

And later at the theater, seeing Jack Malamud lead Ms. G. to their seats with his hand touching her spine, I concoct all kinds of dramas happening between them. He's dying of a terminal illness and she wants to marry him anyway and he refuses. Or he's crazy about marrying her, but she has a sick mother who won't leave Cleveland.

Mostly I wish I had the nerve to tell her what a turmoil I'm in concerning Vic and Matt.

The most extraordinary experience of the day, however, happens while we are taking our seats for the show, about ten minutes before the curtain is due to go up. My seat is on the aisle, so it's easy for Nadine when she grips my hand breathlessly, out of nowhere, and blurts into my ear, "You've got to help me, Trisha!"

There's panic in her eyes and I can't say no. I follow her to the back of the theater. She's trembling. "I just feel you're the only one I can turn to."

I feel like saying, "How come you can't turn to Matt?" But the helpless look on her face stops me.

"It's my father! He's here, Trisha! Third-row orchestra. I just want to run, Trisha!"

"Your father?"

"I haven't seen him in five years. He probably wouldn't even recognize me. He lives in Paris since he divorced my mom. Sends me a letter once a year. Oh, Trisha, what do I do?"

"Do you *want* to talk to your father?"

"No! Yes! Oh, Trisha! He's with a woman! I can't just walk up and introduce myself. Hello, Dad, I'm your daughter, Nadine, remember me? Then suppose we don't have anything to say to each other? I mean, what do you talk about in a situation like this? Oh, Trisha, it's horrible!"

"Then don't do anything."

"Suppose he recognizes me?"

"You said he wouldn't. If he does, let *him* make conversation."

"But if I don't talk to him I'll always feel like a...a...an emotional cripple or something, not having the guts to talk to my own *father*."

"Okay! Go to it! Catch him before the curtain goes up!"

"I can't. Not alone. Will you come with me, Trisha?"

For some reason a spurt of bitterness jumps in me. "You're with Matt, take Matt with you."

"Please, Trisha?"

The house lights dim. "There's no time."

"Promise you'll come with me to meet him and his...his...in the intermission?"

How I'd love to say no. "Okay, okay."

Well, it turns out the play is not so great in the first act, a lot of talk-talk-talk about Life and Death and What-Does-It-All-Mean, but the real-life play that starts in the intermission is a complete grabber.

First we follow the crowd outside, and Matt stays at a distance with his friends because Nadine is clutching my arm like I'm a life preserver.

On the sidewalk the fresh air wakes me up, and I'm wondering when and how I'll see Vic.

"Trisha! Trisha Sargent!" Vic elbows through the crowd toward us, calling my name. His makeup is gone and he's wearing a blue-checked sport jacket and gray pants.

"Trisha, this is great!" Vic makes sure everybody hears him as he takes my hand, and I notice Matt—horsing around with Fat Jack and Pompadour Teddy—give Vic a quick once-over.

"You don't remember me, do you?" Vic goes on loudly. "I met you last Christmas at your cousin's house, when I was visiting Cleveland. I was the one who got you angry because I said Picasso was such a fake. Vic Uris, remember?"

"Oh, yes. Vic. Sure. Hi!" I am absolutely sure that everyone realizes immediately the phoniness of my act, but when I glance at Nadine she seems to take it for real.

"What are you doing in New York, Trisha?"

"A class trip."

"We gotta get together!"

"Uh, Vic, this is Nadine Jorgensen, a classmate of mine."

Vic nods, but Nadine doesn't see it, because she spots her father and her eyes beg me to follow her.

"I'll be right back, Vic."

Uncomprehending but willing, he says, "I ain't gonna move even my little toe."

I quickly whisper in his ear, "Please don't say ain't. It embarrasses me."

He laughs and shakes a finger at me as I follow Nadine through the crowded sidewalk. "I say, old girl, the King's English, eh, wot!"

Sliding past a dozen different conversations, I berate myself for mentioning Vic's "ain't." What right do I have to ask him to speak differently? None. Trisha, you're uptight because he's meeting your friends, and it's not so terrible wanting him to make a good impression.

Then we are standing in front of Nadine's father, a tall square-shouldered blond-bearded hunk arguing heatedly in French with a tall, chic, sultry lady in a peacock blue sheath, pearl necklace, belt of pearls, spike heels, heavy violet eye shadow, and hot pink lipstick.

Nadine suddenly starts to retreat, sees my disapproving face, turns again to face her father squarely and coughs a few times to catch his attention, but he and the woman are deep in some controversy, gesticulating dramatically.

"Excuse me, please." Nadine's voice shakes like a leaf.

"Yes?" Her father breaks off his debate unwillingly and stares down at Nadine.

"Uh..."

The father and his woman exchange puzzled glances.

"Do you know the time, sir?"

He snaps his wrist smartly forward to expose a wafer-thin gold watch. "Nine-thirty, on the dot."

"Thank you." Nadine's eyes fall to the pavement as she turns away and slips past me.

The last I see of her father he is kissing the tip of his companion's nose. The warning buzzer sounds for the second act.

"I'm sorry, Trisha. I didn't have...I couldn't go through with it."

"You tried."

"You think I'm ridiculous, don't you?"

"No."

"Thanks, anyway." Nadine disappears into the theater.

On the sidewalk under the marquee only strangers and Vic remain.

"I ain't"—Vic bows from the waist—"gonna say 'ain't' no more, Pocahontas, except when you and me is alone."

"I apologize, Vic. How you talk is up to you. I actually sometimes like your street talk, but when I thought you were going to meet my friends I suddenly got just like my mother does when Dad starts talking with his old army buddies."

"Listen, I happen to enjoy it when you try to improve my speech."

Just then the warning buzzer sounds again for the second act curtain.

"I've got to be inside, Vic."

"I'm going with you."

"You have a seat?"

"No, but this is the only way I can afford seeing a

play. Of course, I never get to see the first act."

"It's cheating."

"Yeah, sort of, but who does it hurt? There's always an empty seat here and there."

"Do me a favor. Just tonight, don't sneak in. You can meet us outside again and pretend you saw the play."

"Wow, you really are trying to reform me!"

"I guess I am."

"Is that a hopeful sign?"

"Hopeful for what?"

"Hopeful for *us*, Trisha."

We're alone under the marquee. "I don't know, Vic." I kiss him quickly on the mouth and hurry back into the theater. His face seems . . . distant.

Do you have any idea what you're doing, Trisha? Not really.

Sitting through the rest of the play turns out to be torture. When the curtain goes down on the last act there is only scattered polite applause and one curtain call.

Our spirits dampened by the dullness of the play, we gather outside on the sidewalk. Nadine, with Matt at her side, says, "You're a good friend, Trisha."

Matt looks completely puzzled.

I almost burst out, Nadine, you and I will never be good friends! No way! But when I think of her father not even recognizing her I hold my tongue.

"There you are!" Vic dashes up and loops his arm through mine. "Introduce me to your friends, Trisha!"

Well, I introduce him as a friend of my cousin, and he shakes hands with Ms. G. and Jack M. and Ruth and Toni and Nadine and Matt. When Vic and Matt grip each other's hands I half-expect a bolt of lightning.

Heading across Eighth Avenue for coffee and dessert, we're badrapping the play, except for Vic and Matt who seem to be talking about sports and the Olympics.

There's a chill in the street and the coffee shop windows are fogged with steam. Neatly, Vic manages to get himself seated at the table between me and Matt, the two of them quickly discovering that they are both addicted to baseball trivia.

"What did they nickname the Philadelphia Phillies during World War II?"

"Who was the outfielder for the Giants who used to do handstands on the tip of his bat?"

Is Vic purposely cooking up a phony friendship with Matt? Why?

While the boys talk baseball I sit there feeling about as interesting as a bowl of yesterday's Wheaties.

21

"THEY DON'T LIKE you."

"Who?"

"Kiku, Fish, Efren."

"Why?"

"They don't *like* you, they *love* you."

We're sitting in the middle of the Brooklyn Bridge. On the pedestrian walkway above the traffic. Blue East River underneath us prickled with whitecaps. We're watching two figures race away on a moped. The driver is Efren. The passenger is Ruth. The two figures dwindle. The sun is two P. M. April warm minus clouds.

"Ruth is unhappy about Herman."

"Who's Herman?"

"Her guy back in Cleveland."

Occasionally a jogger, walker, skater, two adolescent boys, a skinny man with humped back and corncob pipe, two ten-speed bicycles straddled by bare-legged showgirl types Vic hardly glances at go by, all crossing from Brooklyn to Manhattan or vice versa. And seagulls.

"We don't argue, Vic."

"That's true."

"Not one argument."

"Do you think we should argue?"

"I always argue."

"How come not with me?"

"You're different."

He spices his face with a smile, not quite grateful, not quite embarrassed, a riddle of a smile.

"Maybe it would help our relationship if we argued."

"I *like* not arguing, Vic!"

"I bet I could be good at it if I tried."

"Oh *you*!"

A gust of wind skews his hair forward. I comb my fingers through the unruly golden tangles. The air smells of the sea and car exhaust. Below us we can see tugboats nudging loaded barges upstream. Vic points out Buttermilk Channel, a ribbon of silver water between Governor's Island and the Brooklyn Heights promenade, black-hulled freighters tied up at the docks. In the opposite direction, Manhattan, City Hall, the silver profiles of the World Trade Center, the Justice Building topped by a gold-winged lady, and farther north the landmark Empire State building, the deco Chrysler building, the rectangular pancake U.N. And seagulls.

"Are seagulls happy?"

"Seagulls don't have to be happy."

"Why?"

"I can't explain it. I guess they are exactly who they're supposed to be."

"And we aren't, Vic?"

He shakes his head, the sunlight dancing in the wavy flames of his hair. "Not yet, anyway."

We're sitting on a steel horizontal in the concrete space formed by upright girders where steps raise the pedestrian walk to a higher level.

"*I'm* happy, Vic."

"How happy?"

"About this"—I spreadeagle my arms—"much."

"But not a hundred percent, right, Trisha?"

"Probably. Are you ever a hundred percent happy?"

"Never."

"Think it's possible?"

"Suppose I asked you to stay here, in New York?"

The shock of what he says ricochets around under my ribs.

"I couldn't. No way."

"You don't want to."

"I'm not . . . ready."

"No one's ever ready."

"This is a ridiculous conversation, Vic. I'm not even seventeen. I don't graduate till June. I—"

"Would you like to live here?"

"Even if I were absolutely sure I wanted to be here, I couldn't just decide to stay *now*. It would be like running away from home."

"Do you want to live at home or do you want to go away when you graduate?"

"I guess I want to be on my own. I think."

"So why wait? My mother was only sixteen when she got married."

The word *married* floats between us like a piece of paper twisting and turning in a draft of air.

"You could stay here, work with us on our theater. We need an artist. You'd have a great time, Trisha."

"I think I would."

"We'd all help each other."

"My folks would have the police after me."

"Never find you in Manhattan. Kiku rents a room, I bet she'd flip out to have you be her roommate, split the rent."

"It could be wonderful. Even if it's too late to get accepted into a school here for September, I could start school in Cleveland or Dallas and then transfer to a school in New York in January."

"That sounds sensible, but it ain't gonna happen. See that seagull, it could be the one you named Miracle. Sensible people don't give nicknames to birds they'll never see again. You ain't gonna get a miracle by being sensible."

Far upstream, almost out of sight, the tugboat and its two barges are about to disappear around a bend in the river.

"Close your eyes, Trisha, will you? Please?"

I drop my eyelids until all I see are flashing colors, yellow and green and red.

"Where are you, Trisha?"

"I'm on the Brooklyn Bridge."

"Wrong."

"Then where am I?"

"If you could be anywhere you choose, where would you most like to be in the world?"

The silence feels like we're both in the bottom of a huge wrecked ship.

"I'd most like to be . . . with Vic Uris on the Brooklyn Bridge, or anywhere else he was."

He doesn't answer. My eyes are still closed. I hear him breathing funny and clearing his throat. I open my eyes. His face is turned away from me. He rubs the back of his hands roughly into his eyes, and laughs gruffly.

"What's the matter, Vic?"

I see the remnants of tears in his eyes.

"Nothing. I bit my tongue."

"That's not true."

Vic is silent.

My hand—afraid to be rejected, ready to take flight— lingers on the soft turquoise sleeve of his shirt.

"I don't think in all my life I've ever seen a man . . . cry."

He laughs if off, a dead laugh. "I'm sorry."

"No! No, it's *beautiful*, Vic!"

I rope my arms around his body and crush close to him.

"But you know, Vic, I can't possibly stay here. I have to go back. This time."

"Sure."

"Maybe after graduation—it's only a few more months—I could..."

And we sit there a long time, waiting for Ruth and Efren and Kiku and Fish to come back. They are bringing stuff to have a picnic. A picnic in the middle of the Brooklyn Bridge.

My hand finds Vic's hand. He's looking out toward the haze over Buttermilk Channel. His face seems so strong, so crowded with mysteries. Why am I holding back from him? If I could let go, I think I'd just become part of him and he me. We'd get lost in each other. It could be wonderful. Why don't I?

Sailboats pass beneath the bridge where we sit, the curving white sails broken by the network of steel girders and beams through which we see them. It's all unreal. I think I could sit here in the sunlight with Vic until the end of time.

Maybe I'm a hundred percent happy right now, and maybe Vic is someone you find only once in a lifetime. The road not taken, like Ms. Garfield?

It's scary.

Or will I even remember today at all, say twenty years from now? It seems so world-shaking now, but who knows? Will I remember Jerome the bellhop this morning bursting with the news that he won two thousand dollars gambling in Atlantic City and now he plans to gamble that money on a sure-thing hot tip at the track that'll give him the money he needs to start his shoe store?

Will I remember skinny Miss Carter looking almost pretty, deep in serious conversation with Mr. Kratz, the assistant hotel manager, before we all took off for the Whitney Museum of American Art this morning?

Will I remember how hard Ms. Garfield kept trying to sound cheerful all morning? Or the relief in her eyes when she told us coming out of the Whitney Museum that the rest of the day was ours to wander around on our own in the art galleries and ritzy stores like Saks and Tiffany's and Bergdorf Goodman and Gucci?

Will I remember how Toni said she had a surprise for us and took Ruth and me to meet Peter Parker over on Park Avenue in his slick new Triumph sports car, waiting for her, and the intimate way she kissed him through the car window? Will I remember the poisonous anger in her eyes when she told me to stay out of her life because I took her aside and warned her not to go off with him?

Will I remember Ruth asking to come with me when I told her I wanted to head off on my own, and how downcast she looked when she admitted she had called a friend we knew in Cleveland to ask if Herman had been dating anyone else, and the friend had told her she saw Herman with a snazzy girl, a stranger who didn't go to Patrick Henry? And my explaining to Ruth my whole thing with Vic, from the first day when I threw money in his hat until today having a date with him and his friends on the Brooklyn Bridge?

Will I remember Ruth throwing caution to the winds and mounting the moped behind Efren?

Will I remember Vic right this minute taking my head in his hands and saying quietly, "Why do I feel so good with you, Pocahontas?"

Well, the next few hours on the bridge all rush together, it seems, Ruth and Efren returning, Fish balancing Kiku on a ten-speed bike while her seeing-eye dog jogs alongside, their backpacks disgorging cheese, bread, soda, hard-boiled eggs, tunafish salad, salami, and all our laughter scrambled up with singing and eating and Kiku's fingers dancing across her guitar strings, other people staring or smiling at our oddball picnic.

Until the day suddenly breaks into terrible pieces, like a lovely painted porcelain dish crashing against a wall.

The old couple. The two hoodlums. Vic. The knife. The blood.

First the old couple. The old man walks slowly but erect, proud, leaning heavily on a cane; the old woman, slightly stooped, handbag over her thin shoulder, thick white hair braided around her head, fingers twined around the old man's free arm. They sure look as if they shouldn't be attempting to walk across the bridge. They listen to our singing; she smiles, he winks at us. They move on toward Brooklyn. We forget them so quickly, into our own thing.

Then a scream. The old woman. Two thugs. One pulling at her handbag, she won't let go, dragging her. The other punching the old man, who has a fistful of the thug's shirt.

Vic is the first to see it. The rest of us are frozen for a moment. In that moment Vic is flying at the two muggers. A thought whizzes through me, how much he and Matt are alike. One of the guys swings a club, Vic dodges and kicks him in the ribs and the guy falls. The other guy holding the torn pocketbook slashes at Vic with a knife. Vic blocks the knife with his forearms. The mugger sees Efren and Fish bearing down. Both guys run.

And the blood. Vic's wrist slashed to the bone, blood gushing out. Efren rips off his own t-shirt, balls it up, and forces it against the wound to stanch the flow of blood. Vic's other arm gashed twice but the cuts not so deep, the stain seeping dark down his shirt front and pants.

"Fish, come back! Call the police! Forget those scum! Get Vic on the moped! He's losing blood! What hospital? Hurry! Oh, Vic!"

22

HE TILTS HIS head as I enter the room. His mouth forms the word *hello* silently, and the word seems to glide across the other three beds like one of Efren's paper planes.

He's sitting up in a bed near the window, both arms swathed in snowy bandages. The other patients in the room ignore us.

"For vott you are lookink, young vooman?" Vic beckons me forward with a jerk of his head, his voice deep and authoritarian. "You are being the reporter from the New York Dimes?" he adds, without even a sliver of a smile.

"Uh, yes, that's me! Right!" I fish out a pencil and my sketch pad, standing with my legs pressed against his hospital bed. "My city editor had to pull me off a less important story I've been writing, on the mating habits of alligators in the New York City sewer system."

"Mating, shmayting! The fate ov the entire ceevilized vorld depants on vat you write on *me*!"

"Yes, sir! I've been dying to write something on you!"

I whip out my pen, hold Vic's head gently with one hand, and with the other hand I glide my ballpoint pen across the skin of his cheek.

"Vott are you writink on my chick?"

"T-R-I-S-H-A."

"Do you realize," he whispers, minus the Slavic accent, "we haven't gotten a single laugh from anybody in this room?"

I whisper back, "Either *they're* too sick to laugh, or *we're* too sick to be laughed at."

A touch of pain creases his face for an instant, but he quickly rearranges his features in a smile.

"Your arms, Vic?"

"I guess the anesthesia is wearing off. It's nothing."

"Nothing? You lost so much blood you went into shock!"

"It's nice to see you worry about me."

"I'm not worrying. I just want to be sure that from now on you put your *shocks* where they belong, in the laundry."

A grin seams his face. "Doctor says I'll be out tomorrow. How about the old couple?"

"Lots of bruises, but otherwise they're both okay. Thanks to you. Oh, Vic, when I saw that knife, I was terrified."

"I didn't have time to be scared, it happened without thinking. I'm a lot more scared about..."

"What?"

"Losing you."

"I might always turn up at the lost and found."

He talks into an invisible microphone: "Agent X4Z to Lost and Found. Do you read me? Has anyone found the Blue Mouse? Repeat, has anyone found the Blue Mouse?"

Our smiles draw us close to each other, closer than a kiss, even though we are a foot apart.

"Vic, don't look at me that way, please."

"Why not?"

"It makes me feel...shy."

"That's how *I* feel."

"I can't imagine you shy, Vic."

"With you I am."

"You don't act it."

"Will I see you tomorrow?"

"Of course."

"What about your teacher?"

"I'll find a way."

I kiss him. Not a friendly kiss. Not a sisterly kiss. Not a kiss that makes you tremble.

"That's nice."

"Sure is."

We kiss again. It's the kind of kiss that flows back and forth until you don't know which of you is which and for a moment you don't care.

Back in the waiting room Kiku's seeing-eye dog perks up as I enter, and Kiku and Efren and Fish fire questions at me about Vic. After I answer them, Kiku asks to speak with me alone in the corridor outside.

"When do you leave for Cleveland, Trisha?"

"You sound so serious."

"I am. I'm worried about Vic. Vic and you. Trisha, will you ever see him again after you go home?"

"I care about Vic very very much."

"Boys always look so strong, but they're not. Vic has no one, only us, but we can't hurt him the way you can."

"I don't want to hurt him."

"I believe you, Trisha."

"Thanks."

"Trisha, can I see your face?"

"See?"

Her fingers reach out into empty air, toward my face. I take her hands and bring them toward me. Slowly, she traces the pads of her fingers over my chin, lips, nose, cheeks, eyes, forehead, hair.

"Thank you, Trisha."

I reach my arms around her. She accepts them. We hold each other without words.

Then I am alone in the waiting room. Where's Ruth? The others told me she went to make a phone call. I hate being alone here. Blue smoke rises from a cigarette attached to a slender woman who stands facing the window and hugging herself. She bites her nails and drags on the cigarette and bites her nails and drags, without stopping except to hug herself. A sign on the wall says NO SMOKING.

Hurry up, Ruth, I don't want to be here alone with this woman, too much depression; some people even with their back turned reek of hopelessness, and you feel yourself getting dragged down by them. Plus I hate the smell of cigarettes.

Ruth is calling Herman, I'll bet, and he's probably explaining why he was seen with another girl. He's probably apologizing. Don't apologize, Herman! Be strong! Ruth is a wonderful friend, but don't let her dominate you! What counts is helping each other be happy.

But how do you do that? Does Vic know? He seems so young and so old at the same time, so rough and yet so poetic, so rich with friends and so lonely. Wouldn't he find a way to reach out to this woman in the waiting room biting her nails and puffing her hateful cigarette smoke?

"Trisha, I'd like to talk with you."

I turn to see Ms. Garfield. Ruth is behind her. Ms. Garfield has a very I'm-here-to-help-you look. Ruth's lower lip quivers.

"Ruth called me. Don't be angry with her. She's explained about you and Vic. She—"

"Trisha," Ruth interrupts, her words tumbling nervously over each other, "I'm so afraid you'll do something you'll be sorry for, I had to—"

Anger I've rarely felt suddenly fills me, and I bite into my words savagely as if each one is an enemy: "Ruth, I *trusted* you!"

"I *had* to call Ms. Garfield, Trisha. I was afraid you
might decide to stay in New York."

"You *had* to! You *had* to! Get out of here, Ruth!
Leave me alone!"

Ruth turns white and spins back from Ms. Garfield
toward the door.

"Wait at the hotel, Ruth. I'll meet you there." Ms.
Garfield speaks to the empty doorway where Ruth has
disappeared.

The woman at the window, eyes like blue and white
saucers, stubs out her cigarette and stamps past me with
the words, "Hang in there, honey!"

I take her place at the window, with my back to Ms.
Garfield. I almost wish I enjoyed nailbiting and smoking
so I could pretend to be the other woman.

"We have to talk, Trisha."

"I'd rather not."

"Where did you meet this boy Vic?"

"On the street."

"Did he . . . pick you up?"

"He performs magic and pantomime, to earn money."

"And he asked you for your phone number?"

"No. *I* called *him*."

"Trisha, have you been seeing him often?"

"Yes."

"You've been sneaking away to see him?"

I nod my head. My eyes are burning with the hatred
I feel that Ms. Garfield would question me just like all
the rest of them do when you don't live up to their
expectations.

"How involved are you?"

"Very."

"Does he use drugs?"

"No."

"Have you been with him at night?"

"Yes."

"After bedcheck?"

"Yes."

"All night?"

"Yes."

"Where did he take you?"

"The Staten Island ferry."

"All night?"

I nod yes.

"Anywhere else?"

"I helped them paint their theater near Second Avenue."

"They?"

"Vic and his friends."

"Who are they?"

"Why are you asking me all these questions? He's in the hospital! He's hurt! Isn't that enough for you?"

"Trisha, it's my responsibility to determine what kind of people you've gotten involved with."

"You make it sound so *ugly*. You question me like I'm a criminal or something."

"I'm the one who has to answer if anything happens to you. I'm just trying to do my job."

"Well, leave me alone! I haven't hurt anybody!"

"Who do you think you *are*, Trisha? Every other student has to obey the rules, but not *you*, is that it?"

"I thought you were my friend."

"There are *rules*, Trisha! You've got to have some respect for the rules. What do I know about these people you're involved with? A picnic on the Brooklyn Bridge? A knife fight! A boy in the hospital all slashed? Did he think about *you* when he got you to sneak out at night? You've got to have some sense of responsibility! You've got to handle your life *intelligently*!"

For the first time I raise my voice at her: "Are *you* handling *your* life so intelligently?"

"Why, you impertinent little . . . I ought to—"

Ms. Garfield stops dead. Her fist freezes in midair with the index finger stabbing toward me threateningly.

She drops her fist, unclenching the fingers. She passes her hand across her face. Her voice, after a moment of silence, sounds broken and uncertain.

"I'm sorry, Trisha. I sound like a...like a...*teacher*. Going on at you. Making dumb speeches. I haven't even tried to find out what *you* feel and think."

"And you haven't trusted me. Even though I was wrong to sneak out."

"That's rubbing salt in the wound, but you're right. And you're right about me passing judgment on you while my own feelings are certainly a bit of a mess since I've been here."

With a sigh she sits down on the plastic sofa and presses one hand to her eyes. "I am sorry, Trisha."

"So am I. Maybe I should have told you days ago about Vic, but I didn't want to share him with anyone."

"I know the feeling."

"What do we do now, Ms. Garfield?"

"I'm not sure." She puts out her hand. My hand meets hers.

I can imagine her years ago when Jack Malamud asked her to marry him, and instead she shook herself loose from him and left New York.

And though I know it's madness, for the first time the thought enters my mind that maybe I just might never go back to Cleveland.

23

THE PEN IN my hand springs a leak, black ink spreading over my fingers and smearing the document I'm about to sign. I cock my head with a queasy excuseful smile at Ms. G. who hands me another copy to sign. This time, as I press the nib of the pen into the paper, the pen shatters, spewing ink over both of us. I feel a sickly smile stretch my face, and a laugh bubbles out of my mouth in yellow and red balloons. Then I realize that Ms. G. is actually the Statue of Liberty with a front tooth missing. Matt, no bigger than a bee, wearing a red bathing suit, clings like a mountain climber in the gap between her teeth, and he narrowly misses getting chomped in two as the huge razor-sharp teeth clash together again and again.

I wake up.

Nadine snores blissfully. Ruth, head back, lips apart, breathes in and out with a hushing sound. Sandwiched between two pillows, Toni's face is reduced to the tip of her nose and several wiggles of thick tawny hair.

Toni still isn't talking to me. I'm not talking to Ruth. Ruth isn't talking to Toni because Toni isn't talking to me. And Nadine is the only one everyone is talking to.

The day after tomorrow a busdriver will navigate us back to the shores of the Dead Sea at Patrick Henry High, and people in Cleveland will look at me without even noticing that *inside* a fuse is burning and magical things have happened.

I have no doubt life will go on. Herman Katzenellenbogen will satisfactorily explain everything to Ruth and they will be lovey-dovey again.

Toni will forgive me for mistrusting Peter Parker, just like I will forgive Ruth. Last night when I came back from visiting Vic in the hospital, Nadine told me that Toni had admitted she lent fifty dollars to Peter Parker. Oh, brother! And Toni will, I'm sure, back in Cleveland, continue her search for Mr. Right.

Nadine and I will probably—because we shared the meeting with her father that way—work our way uphill into a friendship.

Matt and I will . . . what? Not the way it was before, certainly. Or could we?

Or is it possible I will call my parents and dare to ask them to send me money to live in New York? Miss my graduation? Not a chance!

Not a chance, Trisha?

Staying in New York would mean the end of absolutely everything for me and Matt. But hasn't it ended already?

And it would be a real beginning for Vic and me. But what's the rush? Why can't we wait till after graduation?

Somehow I think we both know if I leave now, I'm not coming back. I can't explain it.

They always taught me I've got to do what's right. Who's they, anyway? My parents, teachers, friends, books, magazines, even television.

What do you do when you can't figure out what's right? And you don't want to take anybody else's word for it? I guess you just do whatever is next on the agenda.

Like taking Vic home from the hospital.

His friends wanted to help, but I asked if I could be alone with him. I want to give us a chance to see what happens with each other.

In the cab we don't say much. His hands and arms, the bandages all white, lay so stiff and still on his lap.

It's almost as if we're both afraid to brush against each other or meet each other's eyes.

"My hands and arms remind me of a couple of hero sandwiches out in the snow too long." He grins.

"Well, hero hands for a hero!"

The cab veers downtown on Seventh Avenue, across Canal Street, then right on North Moore Street, left on Greenwich, a glimpse of the Hudson River.

"Trisha?"

"Yes?"

"Hello."

After I open the cab door for him and after I unlock the door to his mother's apartment, we're standing in the kitchen and we seem so awkward together, so I get busy and check out his refrigerator instead of standing there tongue-tied.

"This cheese has a bad case of acne."

"That was once a cheese fit for kings."

"Talking about kings, this bread looks like it was found buried with King Tut."

"Please don't badrap my bread."

"Brown milk?"

"There are leprechauns in the refrigerator."

Vic sits quietly at the kitchen window, alternately watching me take stock of what needs to be done and then staring at the boat traffic on the nearby Hudson River.

"Your teacher know you're here?"

"Yes."

Tired, listless, he doesn't seem like the same person. It's almost as if we've both *shrunk* somehow, and don't quite fit the way we did before.

But when I go shopping for him I get a special kick out of learning about the area he lives in. Tribeca, a district in the midst of change, has buildings a hundred years old, small factories, food processors, whole-salers—one by one being recycled into expensive con-dominiums, outdoor cafes, art galleries, boutiques, health food stores. To the west is the Hudson River, where a landfill project has left acres of sand dunes. South is the looming silver geometry of The World Trade Center, and all of Wall Street nearby, plus Chambers Street boiling over with army surplus and bargain hunter stores, artist's lofts—you could spend months roaming around. Years.

And my favorites, a street that smells of spices, a street that smells of cheeses, and a street that smells like a river of freshly roasted coffee.

"Trisha, don't bother with all that shopping!"

"Vic, be a good boy."

I haul his laundry to a kookie laundromat where there are tables and chairs and fascinating art magazines for the customers to browse in and a stock of refrigerated yogurt for sale, loads of artists and dancers and theatrical-type people with laundry.

In the apartment itself an irresistible urge wells up in me to clean, fix, dust, wash, mop, scrape—things I normally fight to avoid at home.

"Cut it out, Trisha!"

"No! This refrigerator probably hasn't been cleaned since the War of 1812."

"Well, I like things the way they are!"

"Sorry, you'll just have to live with a little cleanli-ness."

"You don't understand, Trisha. If things aren't messy, it doesn't feel like home."

"Home is where the dirt is, huh? I don't believe you."

"Calling me a liar?"

"Maybe I am and maybe I'm not."

We both at the same time realize we are raising our voices, and we stop dead. Slowly, grudgingly, we make I'm-sorry faces, and I go back to my cleaning.

"Oh, no! Not the windows!"

"Why not?" I brandish the Windex.

"If I start seeing what's outside those windows, I'll get very depressed."

"*You!*" I retaliate with a squirt of Windex across his shirt.

"You're lucky I've been wounded in battle or I'd put you over my knee."

"You wouldn't dare."

"Stick around a few weeks, when my arms are healed."

The idea of what our lives will be like in a couple of weeks shuts us both up.

I wonder if he will ask me again to stay in New York.

But even if there is a way for me to work it out, do I want to?

When I start to leave the apartment—Ms. Garfield said I could help out Vic until the late afternoon—we haven't talked about anything that mattered. And I'm glad.

We don't even kiss, we throw each other a small wave of the hand. We've made no plans for tomorrow, my last full day in Manhattan.

The jukebox in the bar downstairs starts vibrating an old Elvis Presley record up into Vic's kitchen. *"Houn' dawg!"* Going down the steps, I hear the door to his apartment close. I start back up the steps and lift my hand to knock. No, Trisha, don't do it.

I run all the way down the two flights of narrow stairs. Open the street door. Step out onto the sidewalk.

Someone I know stands staring at the apartment buzzers, which are on the street wall because the building is so ancient it doesn't even have a lobby.

Someone I know screws his eyes up close to the nearly

illegible names on the buzzers, only six apartments in the whole building.

The person I know is Matt. He doesn't look at all surprised to see me. I'd like to blurt out, "What are *you* doing here?" I'd also like to tell him how handsome he looks, how angry I am at him for going out with Nadine, how guilty I feel about secretly seeing Vic while we were going steady, how scared I feel about losing him and also about losing Vic, how beautiful I feel about feeling—and how awful I feel about feeling.

Instead of all that, I don't say anything.

Matt says, "I didn't mean to meet you. Sorry."

"That's okay. We're not exactly mortal enemies."

"Which buzzer is his?"

"Apartment two, top of the first landing, door to the right."

"Thanks."

"Matt?"

"Yes?"

"Why are you here?"

"That's a good question, Trisha."

"I'm full of good questions lately."

"How about answers?"

Is that a trickle of a smile on his face? One little raindrop of a smile? The two of us fidget a moment.

"Well, I guess I'll be going, Matt."

"Hey, you know how you can always tell that your child is growing up?"

"How?"

"When he stops asking where he came from, and starts refusing to tell where he's going."

His eyes are drilling into my profile. I can feel it as I turn to go, and I wish I could tell him we are both very funny, but I can't because I never knew before this moment how laughter is the other side of sadness.

24

NIBBLING AT MY finger through the bars of his cage, a long-haired mountain goat looks up at Vic and me with eyes that seem so *yearning*.

Maybe what we really want to say to each other, Vic and I, will never get said.

A bright silver heart balloon filled with helium tugs at the string in my other hand as if the tops of the trees are luring it toward the cloudless April sky that seems to bend low over the outdoor cages of the zoo.

"Bite, please?"

Vic holds his mouth toward a huge hot salted pretzel in my hand. I allow him a generous bite. He chews diligently. I enjoy his pleasure.

"What time tomorrow, Trisha?"

"Ten A.M. You'll be there?"

"Doubt it."

"I wish you would."

"I'd rather not."

A buffalo the color of mud evaluates us from behind the black iron verticals of his backyard.

"Your arms don't hurt?"

"Not really."

"Will there be any permanent injury?"

"No."

Around the corner from the buffalo, a tawny coyote gives us the cold shoulder and turns his back disdainfully as we draw near.

"Matt visited you yesterday."

"Right."

"Were you going to tell me, Vic?"

"Not unless you asked. Are you asking?"

"Not really."

Vic and I are talking, but the words don't touch what is most us.

A polar bear floats on his back in a pool of greenish water, oblivious to us.

"Will you say goodbye to Kiku for me?"

"Sure."

"And Fish?"

"And Efren."

"Thanks, Vic."

"They'll miss you."

"I'll miss them too."

A slick wet seal barks on a rock, claps its flippers, dives into the green water, speeds underwater like a phantom shadow.

"How's your friend Toni?"

"I think she's having a rough time. We're still not talking."

"Why?"

"Neither of us wants to be first, I guess. It's bizarre. Four of us in one room and three of us not talking."

His eyes seem filled with a sort of wry understanding, as if he knows how silly it is and at the same time how hurtful.

"New York"—he hunts for words—"does funny things to people."

"Sometimes not so funny. I heard that Peter Parker got fired. He's the night clerk Toni loaned all her money to because he said he'd pay her back the next day, and he didn't."

Vic stops walking, beckons me to come closer. From one direction there's the sound of birds screeching, from the opposite direction an elephant trumpets, and overhead a clock sounds the hour loudly, musical notes, and animal statues proceed in a circle around the clock.

"I have to show you the most magical place in Manhattan."

His bandaged arms motion me to follow him.

"Are you sure you're not the Pied Piper?"

"I'm not sure of anything these days." He waits for me to catch up with him.

The path curves under a kind of bridge. Up ahead a sign reads: CHILDREN'S ZOO.

"That's where I belong," Vic murmurs. "Kids are born magicians, born mimes."

"Born everything."

The sunlight falling warm through a mass of branches reminds me of millions of tiny goldfish slipping between the twisted strands of a fisherman's net.

"But it's not so great being a kid."

"It's not so great being grownup either."

Absently, Vic touches his bandaged arm to his hair, forgetting that his fingers aren't free to comb through the tangles.

I lay the palm of my hand against his chest. Our bodies are so close. His lips explore my forehead.

"I wish . . ."

"What?" His voice so soft, his eyes glistening into me.

I shake my head.

"Tell me, won't you? What do you wish?"

"I wish I could stop wishing."

Sunlight from behind him creates a sort of halo around the reddish gold of his hair.

"You've got a halo."

"That's me, Saint Victor."

He crinkles his eyes, stoops his shoulders, his face becoming somehow very old and loving, his voice ancient. "Let us pray, my daughter."

"What should we pray for?"

"Ah, that's the problem."

Vic straightens up with a false laugh, becoming himself. "My body is in Manhattan, but I'm somewhere else."

"Where, Vic?"

"Don't you know?"

I shake my head.

"I'm on the way back to Cleveland with you, Trisha."

He reacts to the alarm in my eyes.

"Hey, relax, I'm only kidding. I sure ain't planning to be a stowaway on your bus."

His eyes are so intense I have to look away.

"Can I kiss you?"

"Yes, Vic."

"How many times?"

A grin passes between us as if we were two halves of one face, the very same electrical messages flowing across the very same nerve cells to form one smile on the two of us.

"As many times as you want."

His mouth touches my hair, my forehead, my cheekbones, my eyes, quick little kisses, not stopping, my ears, my neck, my chin, and for a moment I want to pull away, embarrassed, but then I let myself feel the pleasure of it and I start laughing, and Vic, his voice deep, laughs with me.

Then the laughter stops and we seem to be avoiding each other's eyes.

"The bag lady hasn't been around for days." I'm trying to make conversation.

"The *who?*"

"Didn't I tell you about her?"

He shakes his head vaguely. I can see he wants to concentrate on the children's zoo.

"I'll tell you some other time."

We buy two tickets and move through the turnstile. The children's zoo, so small and sweet, just right for even three-year-olds to wander through without a chance of getting lost, makes me laugh with pleasure the moment I glance around.

Sitting and walking, touching and giggling, petting the sheep and the goats and the cows, feeding the ducks, giving our helium-filled heart on a string to a little sobbing girl who stops crying and then lets the silver heart go free high up into a wind that carries the glittering speck far beyond our sight, and then climbing into the turreted castle and Noah's Ark and the white whale and Hansel and Gretel's candy house, I find myself nearer and nearer to tears.

"How does the strawberry taste, Trisha?"

I shake my head.

"The poor guy is hanging from the cliff, the tiger about to attack, the mice chewing the root, and you don't know how the strawberry tastes?"

"How does it taste to *you*, Vic?"

"I can't reach it."

We sit together soaking up sun on a small bench, watching the children roam over Noah's Ark and toddle toward the ducks.

"Was I right about this place?"

"Oh yes, Vic!"

His arm slips awkwardly around my shoulder.

"If you stayed, we could come here any time we want."

We roam away from the children's zoo and toward the heart of Central Park. Joggers, roller skaters, cyclists, soccer players, baby carriages, all reel past us like images on a movie screen, as if only Vic and I are real and the rest of the world is imaginary.

Then carousel music, the oompa rhythm of it, bright clear metallic tunes, reaches for us over the grassy rises and massive thrusts of dark granite.

"Two, please."

My horse, inky black mane flying in the wind, gleaming white teeth, eyes ablaze, charges forward, while Vic, a few feet behind, mounted on a white horse with hooves kicking forward, never catches up to me no matter how many times we race around and around the carousel.

Then walking. In Sheep's Meadow, a spacious grassy area. The crack of a distant baseball bat. A soccer goalie leaping to block a kick. Kites fluttering high up.

"I'd like to be the first."

"First what, Vic?"

"Has anyone ever asked you to marry him?"

"I'm not even seventeen, Vic."

"Matt never asked you?"

"Not really."

"Good. I'm asking. Will you marry me, Trisha?"

"You know I can't."

"At least I'll always be the first guy who asked you."

"Yes."

"I love you."

"Oh, Vic."

We hold each other. I want so much to tell him that I love him too, but . . . my lungs are closed as stone.

"Agent X4Z calling the Blue Mouse! Come in, Blue Mouse!"

"Agent X4Z, this is the Blue Mouse. I read you."

"The strawberry tastes great! I repeat: The strawberry tastes great!"

I lay my hands against his cheeks, cradling his face between the palms of my hands.

"Vic, I'm not so special."

"To me you are. I don't know why. I've been with plenty of girls. But you—you're the first one who makes me know, when I'm with you, how lonely I am when we're not together."

"Is that love?"

His eyebrows and shoulders rise together in a funny question mark.

A tightness under my ribs, hard like a vault of cold iron, softens, eases, warms, opens, and I feel suddenly as if there is so much more space and light inside me.

25

WHEELING WEST ON the Pennsylvania Turnpike. Destination Cleveland, Ohio. There is no joy aboard this bus. Except perhaps in the bosom of the woman driver.

She's cute, petite, bobbed hair under a wide-brimmed cowboy hat, a button nose, high-heeled ranch boots, and she's chewing gum and humming "Deep in the Heart of Texas" as her leather-gloved hands expertly swing the steering wheel.

Why is everybody so depressed? What's the big deal about Manhattan? Maybe it's the thought of two more months trapped in the half-baked halls of Patrick Henry High. Or maybe I'm not the only one leaving something behind that may never be found again.

Ms. Garfield sits near the driver, her eyes closed but not asleep. Did she have the nerve to tell Jack Malamud she loves him? Or did she wait for him to ask her to come back, and he didn't ask? Or did he ask her to marry him at the last minute, and *she* chickened out again?

Everybody seems so separate from everybody else. Even Fat Jack with his bristly haircut and Teddy Jackson with his pompadour are not their usual noisy wise-guy selves. The road signs grow toward us, bigger and bigger, then whip past. Harrisburg. Scranton. Pittsburgh.

159

Matt sits staring through the window in the last row. He's usually chummy and talkative. Not today. What's he thinking? About me? Not likely. But why did he go to visit Vic? He hasn't said a word to Nadine. Why isn't she sitting next to Matt?

And Toni, poor Toni, diagonally across the aisle, her face buried in a magazine. The pages turn, but I bet she's not reading a word. Her eyes—I'd bet anything—are swimming in angry tears. Toni, I hate him with you! He had no right to make such a fool of you.

Ruth now, all I can see of *her* is the back of her head when I stand up. I know she'll welcome me with open arms the moment I talk to her, and in my heart I have already forgiven her for ratting on me, but somehow I still feel like staying away. It's almost as if my talking to Ruth again will be like a betrayal of Vic. Trisha, your brain is bent.

I don't want to betray Vic, not ever.

And there's skinny spinster Miss Carter, for the first time in our whole trip actually chatting away with her niece Marcia, the two of them really friendly. People are such surprises. Why does Miss Carter look so vivacious and young? They have to be the only two of us coming home the least bit happy. Is it connected to the smile I saw on the face of Mr. Kratz, the assistant hotel manager with the unpredictable toupee, when he personally carried Miss Carter's suitcases out of the hotel for her?

It's funny, but why am I suddenly so much more sensitive to other people? People used to be all a blur, unless they were close friends or family. Now I seem to find myself worrying about practically strangers.

Like the bag lady. Like Jerome the bellhop. Like Eleanor Roosevelt. Like Kiku and Efren and Fish. Like Nadine.

What is it about New York or Vic or me or maybe just being near to graduation or so near to falling in love that makes you feel other people's troubles this way?

The petite busdriver blows a chewing gum bubble and swings the bus around a curve as if it were a sports car. The afternoon sun shoots its hot red eye behind a grid of tree trunks and telephone poles. She acts like she doesn't have a worry in the world.

But now I know that everybody alive has troubles, because everybody cares about something or somebody, and if you care you worry.

Jerome the bellhop cares. This morning he told me his younger brother is retarded, but they can't afford the special treatment he needs. Jerome staked all his winnings on a long shot to buy his beloved shoe store so he can take care of his brother. As he helped me carry out my suitcases, Jerome explained how he lost every cent of his winnings, plus other money he had borrowed to bet with.

"Don't come back," he warned me as a goodbye. "This town just chews you up and spits you out!"

And Eleanor Roosevelt cares. I knocked on her door before I left. She took my hand and wished me luck. Her high teased hair wasn't orange anymore. The swirls of her hair were a plain brown. And she had a black eye. "I stopped coloring my hair," she said. She saw me staring at her black eye. "I found him," she said.

"Oh," I gulped. My heart felt like it was being shredded into little pieces.

"Don't worry," she added, her mouth twisting up at the corners in a defiant smile. "He'll change his mind."

And the bag lady. The bag lady cares. She was there on the pavement near the hotel entrance, but across the street this time. She was slowly eating a huge peach, while a rag of a man sat huddled against a wall, hair and hands and face filthy, clothes a mess, feet bare and purpled.

The bag lady tapped the man's shoulder. He looked up at her, blinking. She placed half the peach in his hand. He laid his lips against the peach without biting it. She returned impassively to her own portion of the sidewalk and proceeded to clean her fingernails.

Vic, oh, Vic, I'm missing you already!

And what about Matt? Still staring at the countryside, rolling hills and farmland of Ohio. Thinking what, Matt? Maybe I know in my heart why Matt was there that day to visit Vic.

Cleveland hasn't changed. One person stands waiting on the sidewalk as the bus brakes to a stop. He is holding a handful of flowers wrapped in a cone of green florist tissue paper, plus he has a box of—naturally—chocolates in his other hand. Herman Katzenellenbogen, of course.

Herman and Ruth go off together in her parents' car, casting shy delighted glances at each other and babbling a mile a minute. I think I hear him say, "She was my *cousin!*"

Toni, Matt, Nadine, all split in different directions.

Ms. Garfield stops me. Her face radiates excitement. "Trisha, whatever you do, I hope you'll always count me among your friends. I've decided to call New York and ask him if the two of us can try to make it work!"

She hugs me quick and runs toward the nearest telephone booth.

I grab a cab alone.

26

"YOU LOOK FAMILIAR."

"I do?"

"Yeah, I never forget a—sure! I remember I told my wife about you for laughs. You was in my cab. You forgot to feed Paul Newman! I says to my wife, 'This kid is got a dog or somethin' name of Paul Newman!'"

"He's a cat."

"Dog, cat, parakeet, what's the difference, it's still Paul Newman!" The cabdriver guffaws. He has a round, jowly face, triple chins, bad teeth, and a tough kindly voice that now I remember reminds me of my late grandfather who used to make me feel like the most important person in the world.

"Well, you sure made me laugh, me and my wife, and we sure need it these days."

"What's she like, your wife?"

"My wife? Oh, you asked the right guy! You got a couple hours? I could write a book. She's a diamond. One in a million. She's an angel. I could tell you stories. Why she sticks with a bum like me I don' know."

"You don't look like a bum."

"That's only 'cause I'm so young an' good-lookin'!"

When the cabdriver drops me in front of my house,

I reach out to pay him, but he shakes his head. "This one's on me! Talkin' to you about Harriet took me outta the dumps. You got good ears, kid."

He honks as he pulls away and waves.

I guess there are people who are living alive lives, if you ask the right questions.

Inside my house there's no one home, of course, because both Mom and Dad are at work, but they've hung up a big homemade sign from wall to wall: "WELCOME HOME, TRISHA, DARLING!"

And I realize how much I've been missing them without even knowing it. And suddenly, happily, warmly, I know I'm glad to be home.

For a moment I imagine I'll also find a telegram from Vic, something like:

DEAR POCAHANTAS,
HAPPY STRAWBERRY!
AGENT X4Z

But no telegram. He didn't ask for my Cleveland address. I didn't offer to tell him.

What did I do with his phone number? Left it in the drawer in the HO EL MAN A TAN.

I dial Information, 411, to be sure I can find his number if I want it. The operator says, "What city, please?"

I hang up.

I plan to call Toni tonight and apologize. To call Ruth and apologize. To call Ms. G. and say thanks and congratulations. To call Nadine and ask her over.

Paul Newman leaps up on my lap and rubs his head against my fingers, informing me that he yearns to be scratched behind his ear.

I wonder if that helium-filled silver balloon we gave away at the zoo is hanging limp and empty on the branch of some tree.

There's a knock at the door. I can tell that knock anywhere. My nerves are suddenly on the alert. I'm glad the doorknob feels so familiar and comforting.

"Hi!" My voice sounds awfully squeaky.

"I just want to tell you I want to try again!" he blurts out.

It's a Matt I've never seen before. He looks not so sexy, not so cool, not so smooth talking, not so *together* as he used to be.

But maybe it's not Matt who's changed, maybe it's the way I *look* at him that's different.

"So do I, Matt."

"You *do*?"

That really hits him. I guess there's an awful lot I don't know about that goes on inside him.

"I do want to try again, Matt."

"I thought I'd have to go on a hunger strike or something."

"Can I kiss you, Matt?"

He looks perplexed.

"Trisha, you're . . ."

"What?"

The kiss. I hold him. He holds me. There's friendship in the kiss, friendship and wonderment. I'm not all shaky and stirred up and scared. When I take my mouth away gently, Matt's eyes look troubled.

"Are you okay?"

"Yes, sure. No, I'm not. Trisha, what about Vic?"

I shake my head. "Will you tell me sometime what you two talked about?"

Matt nods, squeezes my hand, walks away. Halfway down the block, he turns, sees me still at the door, and waves.

I wave back.

Maybe we don't have to be hanging from a cliff for a plain ordinary strawberry to taste wonderful.

One Blue Mouse will always be grateful to her Charlie

Chaplin boy. Goodbye, Agent X4Z. Goodbye, Seamus Vittorio Aristotle Rappaport McDonald.

Maybe I don't have to go to exciting new places and meet eccentric, mysterious people to feel the romance that I hunger for.

Maybe the romance is inside me and always ready to be tapped, if I listen and open my eyes and ask the right questions.

When a teen looks for romance, she's looking for

CAPRICE

_____	BEFORE LOVE	16846-4/ $1.95
_____	THE BOY NEXT DOOR	07185-6/ $1.95
_____	A BICYCLE BUILT FOR TWO	05733-0/ $1.95
_____	CARRIE LOVES SUPERMAN	09178-4/ $1.95
_____	DANCE WITH A STRANGER	16983-5/ $1.95
_____	DO YOU REALLY LOVE ME?	16053-0/ $1.95
_____	A HAT FULL OF LOVE	31787-1/ $1.95
_____	HEARTBREAKER	31973-4/ $1.95
_____	HEARTWAVES	31991-2/ $1.95
_____	THE HIDDEN HEART	32908-X/ $1.95
_____	LAST KISS IN APRIL	47119-6/ $1.95
_____	LOVE BYTE	49543-5/ $1.95
_____	LOVE IN FOCUS	49630-X/ $1.95
_____	LOVE NOTES	49702-0/ $1.95
_____	NEVER SAY NEVER	56971-4/ $1.95
_____	A NEW FACE IN THE MIRROR	57122-0/ $1.95

Prices may be slightly higher in Canada.

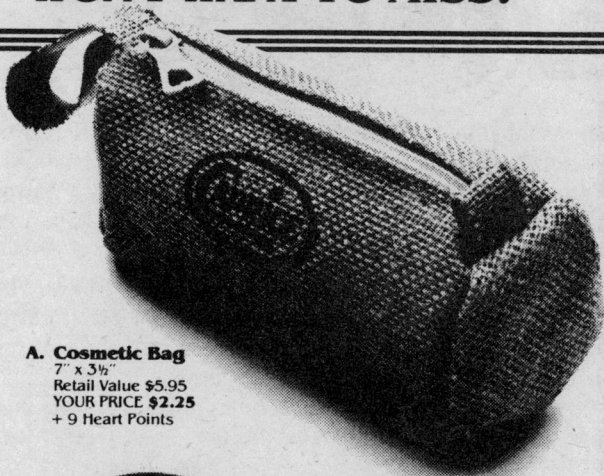

CAPRICE

Now that you're reading the best in teen romance, why not make that *Caprice* feeling part of your own special look? Four great gifts to accent that "unique something" in you are all yours when you collect the proof-of-purchase from the back of any current *Caprice* romance!

Each proof-of-purchase is worth 3 Heart Points toward these items available <u>only</u> from *Caprice*. And what better way to make them yours than by reading the romances every teen is talking about! Start collecting today!

Proof-of-purchase is worth 3 Heart Points toward one of four exciting premiums bearing the distinctive *Caprice* logo

CAPRICE PREMIUMS
Berkley Publishing Group, Inc./Dept. LB
200 Madison Avenue, New York, NY 10016

PROOF OF
PURCHASE
—3—
HEART POINTS
♥ ♥ ♥
DETAILS INSIDE